HOW MY PRANK STORIES IN
'You Tube'
MADE ME AN
OVERNIGHT SENSATION

HOW MY PRANK STORIES IN
'You Tube'
MADE ME AN
OVERNIGHT SENSATION

THE GREATEST STORY TELLER THAT EVER LIVED, WELL ALMOST . . .

JIMMY CORREA

iUniverse, Inc.
Bloomington

**HOW MY PRANK STORIES IN 'YOU TUBE' MADE ME AN OVERNIGHT SENSATION
THE GREATEST STORY TELLER THAT EVER LIVED, WELL ALMOST . . .**

iUniverse books may be ordered through booksellers or by contacting:

iUniverse
1663 Liberty Drive
Bloomington, IN 47403
www.iuniverse.com
1-800-Authors (1-800-288-4677)

ISBN: 978-1-4759-2788-7 (sc)
ISBN: 978-1-4759-2789-4 (ebk)

Printed in the United States of America

iUniverse rev. date: 05/18/2012

I dedicate this book to all my friends in You Tube because without them this could never have come to light; nor could I have gotten the enjoyment I receive from chatting, swapping, and making a fool out of myself through my daily blogs. I love you all and know that you're a part of me forever and a day.

Thank you, Jimmy

Contents

My Acknowledgment

Without my friends this book would have never come to print. It is through my blogging and our chatting and sharing that motivated me to write this book and I want the whole world to know that friendship is a treasure, more valuable than diamonds, pearls, and all the gold in California, it just can't be bought. So please pass it along because we sure can use more camaraderie in this planet we call mother earth. I love each and every one of you.

A lot of my subject material came from my having written three Rock 'N Roll Trivia Books and from my huge music collection. At one point I had a combined total of over 6000 vinyl albums, cassettes, CD's, VHS and DVD's music related movies, autobiographies, and specials. I have been to many concerts to see some of the legends I speak about and it's obvious music is my true passion. I enjoy reading about it from newspapers, magazines including my favorite, Rolling Stone magazine. I was raised on American Bandstand, The Ed Sullivan Show, The Clay Cole Show, Where The Action Is, American Top Ten, and Soul Train. I've listened to XM Satellite Music Radio and enjoy the 50s, 60s, 70s, and 80s. My three favorite dj's were/are Casey Kasem, Wolman Jack, still in syndication, and Rick Dees. The Annual Hall of Fame Induction is a treat to watch and also The American Music Awards, The Grammy's, and The Billboard Awards. I watch American Idol as often as I can, the X-Factor, and all the PBS Music Specials and America's Got Talent. So you see there's never a dull moment in my household not when you got You Tube to fill the void in between. Long live Rock 'N Roll and You Tube.

Jimmy

Introduction

YouTube is an internet web site owned and operated by the giant search engine Google. It was my daughter who introduced me to this phenomenon and at first I was hesitant and leery of it but after a year decided to take a try at it. I didn't want my business out in the public for everybody to see like some other web sites do. My lack of understanding was the primary reason, but once I familiarized myself with the in's and out's I was hooked. I would spend on an average about 3-4 hours a day in You Tube and sometimes even more especially since I had four channels to contend with. My primary purpose was to entertain my friends through my blogs of made up stories and the sharing of my collection of music, movies, TV, and poetry that I would store in various files known as 'Favorites,' and 'Play Lists,' where I could watch as often as I wanted but equally important easily retrieve, update, add, delete, and share with my friends in the network. At one time I had three public viewing channels; dakotajim11378, consisting of all the greatest rock 'n roll music from its inception back in 1955, theloveman11378, which contained all the greatest love ballads I could find and presently the only channel still active today, and jimmyscomedyshop, which encompassed anything funny posted in You Tube. On a daily basis I would go into these channels to communicate with my friends, to post bulletins on what I found interesting and wanted others to see, and to also make new friends. Why you say, because I get personal gratification sharing my awesome collection with friends who I select wisely. Wisely in that we have similarities, are compatible and or interesting. I'm not into rap music, and I don't put it down because I recall when I was a kid how some folks frowned against Elvis and Little Richard who I thought were cool. So those channels of that genre, rap, I tend to avoid. I also avoid channels that are into politics and religion because I have my own personal beliefs and like to keep them private and of my own choosing. I look for those channels that are fun loving, clean cut, and entertaining. I have literally turned down thousands of invites for lack of compatibility. Music is my number one priority and then movies, and finally poetry. Sometimes what captures my attention is that person's profile. It may contain eye catching poetry or a fascinating history of their life style. Also what might capture my attention is their channel's back ground; it may be colorful or inspiring. Many times I come across music that I already have but if it's better than mine I'll copy it because I like only the best. Video makers are another factor that I consider because they are the ones that keep You Tube going. I enjoy rating and making comments on new uploads old or new. I must have personally commented on over 1500 videos and it always gives me pleasure to support these talented individuals who are so artistic and masterful. My philosophy is, if you come across something unique or well done then it pays to comment and that will support and motivate those downloader's to make more and we in You Tube reap its rewards. I don't make videos at the moment I just collect the best that I can find. Sometimes when you do a search out populates various versions. I try to collect the best sounding and most impressive versions. Live recordings are great but if it's a poor copy then I go to the next and sometimes that may just be a record spinning on a record player or on a juke box. It may not look pretty but the sound may be just perfect. These are my guidelines and I only speak for myself, others may have their own agendas so I am not the rule of thumb but I do hope others will choose You Tube as their source of entertainment and for socializing and to be part of this wonderful network

Basic Working Knowledge of You Tube

Please note on March 12, 2012 You Tube underwent a major facelift operation; some features were deleted or changed including the visibility of a person's profile and their comments field which for the most part allowed one to interact on a much quicker pace. And last but not least the ability to send out a bulletin which allowed you to speak to your entire network of friends and subscribers.

An account or channel can be opened up in a matter of a few minutes and free of charge. To do so, you need an e-mail address, create a password that can be changed at any time, and as often as you like, and a channel name, ex. dakotajim123.

When you do any search, a song, movie, TV show, comedian etc. the You Tub system populates a bunch of choices and other related videos and after viewing as many as you like you can save one or more of the choices to your channel as a favorite and or in a playlist that you must create a name for easy access, ex. folk songs, romantic movies, jazz, and so on.

The You Tube system initially allowed a maximum of 650 favorites and within time it will expand allowing you more but there's no set time frame when that will happen. Presently I have 1676 favorites and over 270 playlists. There is a maximum of 200 favorites in a single playlist; but you can create an unlimited number of them.

A video can be saved and shared (sent to others)

You can feature a video on your channel set to play automatically once you or somebody makes a visit

When you create an account or a certain playlist you can set it up as a private or for public viewing. Meaning it can be viewed only by you or whomever you allow to see it, or kept in a public mode for anyone who visits your channel to see.

At any time you can make a comment to a video, with less than 500 characters. Any over that amount will not be allowed until you have reduced the number of words or letters.

You can send a share to one person or a multiple group of people as an e-mail or through other network systems, face book, etc.

You can block anyone who you do not want coming into your channel for whatever reasons

Your in and out messages can be saved or erased at any time

Your comment field can be set up to make and receive comments and can be deleted at any time. You also have the option not to set it up or allow only friends to make comments in your channel or anybody at random and or needing your approvable before it is made public.

You Tube updates on a daily basis your current subscribing numbers. Also every so often the technicians will implement new enhancements to the operating system. For example, a bulletin feature was added about a year or so ago. This was a way for you to post a message that would allow you to make any important announcements to all your friends and subscribers. For example: a new download or a video you want to bring attention to in your network of friends and subscribers. As I stated this feature was deleted on March 12th.

There is a slot on your channel's page called Avatar where you can post your photo or a photo or image that represents your channel's theme.

You Tube does not allow any video download not in line with the laws and conditions set upon by their rules and guidelines. This is to protect artists and owners of their rights that might conflict with their royalties or lack of permission.

A channel can be canceled by You Tube for violations or you can cancel your account at any time you so desire

You Tube has the right to place advertisements on your channels which is how they compensate for this free membership.

Those channels that generate many viewers can get compensated; see the details in You Tube

I hope this helps, there are other rules and more operating functions I have not mentioned. You will learn more once you familiarize yourself with the working system.

My Four Channels on YouTube

dakotajim11378 was created on December 31, 2008 for collecting Rock 'N Roll songs from its inception starting with Bill Haley And His Comets in 1955 who scored the first Rock 'N Roll song according to Billboard called "(We're Gonna) Rock Around The Clock" that was featured in the blockbuster movie 'Blackboard Jungle.' My collection has no limits or boundaries; it includes movies from the silent screen era to the talkies, and those songs from the mid-50s through today's modern day hits and of every genre: pop, rock, country, R&B, Foreign, instrumentals, Broadway hits, folk, the novelties, and the one hit wonders in the top 40 charts. I also have Pre-Rock 'N Roll hits dating back to the 40s and early 50s and some even before that. It is this channel that I've become a wannabe DJ showcasing the very best music out there. Elvis, Connie Francis, The Everly Brothers, The Beatles, The Rolling Stones, Dusty Springfield, Billy Joel, Rod Stewart, John 'Cougar' Mellencamp, Hall & Oates, Linda Ronstadt, Bob Segar, Elton John, Paul McCartney, Pat Benatar, Joan Jett & The Blackhearts, Fleetwood Mac, Heart, The Dobbie Brothers, the Eagles, CCR, Tina Turner, Motown, Atlantic Records, Stax, Celine Dion and so forth and the list keeps growing. And most of all I like sharing them with all my friends, so don't be a stranger come on over and see me some time hahahaha, no this is not May West, it's me Jimmy, your local DJ. Btw there's no admission price but I do ask that you check your knives and guns at the front door cos I don't tolerate violence in my house. The only uproar will be on the dance floor so let's get this party started as soon as you make a visit at any time, 24/7, eight days a week . . .

theloveman11378 was created on November 1, 2009 to collect all the greatest romantic ballads ever known to man from every decade and from every genre. They include the happy ones and the sad ones, better known as the heartbreakers. It may deal with boy meets girl, dating, marriage, breakups, death, a celebration of a holiday, ex. Valentine's Day and so on. Through this channel folks tend to think I'm a player, a womanizer. Well I'm not, just like to pretend, have fun, and share ballads to die for. And yes I love the slow ones, where you hold your partner real tight and just move closer and closer until there's no room for the Holy Ghost. Why am I called the love man, because I've been around the block more times than you can count, thirteen to be exact and three times just to one lady, my shrink, but that's another story for some other time. Let's just say she couldn't get enough of me. Btw her favorite song is "Do It Again" by The Staple Singers; yes she calls me her hammer on the block, hahaha. Enough of me hope you'll enjoy all the comments posted in this section, my romance channel.

jimmyscomedyshop was created on April 1, 2010 with the intent to collect anything funny including but not limited to TV, movies, sitcoms, concerts, jokes, books, and poetry. I also feature the best scenes from all the popular movies including some of the most dramatic ones, Oscar worthy. Some of my favorites include court room summations when actors portraying lawyers give the most impressive speeches to win over the juries. Gregory Peck, Spencer Tracy, Paul Newman, Al Pacino, and Kevin Costner are just a few that come to mind. Through this channel I can post jokes, some are mine and some sent to me by friends. No I don't do standup but if I did, Richard Pryor, Jonathan Winters, Joan Rivers, Rodney Dangerfield, George Carlin, Flip Wilson, and Robin Williams would have been shaking in their boots, hahaha, enjoy.

I have a fourth channel that is private that I created to share with my best friend and may I say she has the prettiest eyes I have ever seen, and she's not only awesome but has made me videos to die for, hahaha, also private, let me say no more . . . Vulgar and sweet!!!

dakotajim11378

Welcome to Jimmy's Sock Hop Channel!

The 50s, 60s, 70s, 80s, 90s & the New Millennium

Yes folks, that's the boy from NYC himself, Jimmy!!!

The majority of this book deals with fictional stories I have written and shared with my friends in You Tube through e-mail blogs intending to put a smile on their faces and maybe even get them to laugh. For the most part these stories were the basis surrounding a song, a movie, or a current event including a holiday such as Mother's Day, Valentines Day or a personal incident that I was involved in or witnessed. They were sent to groups of friends ranging anywhere from one to sixty, some old acquaintances and some new ones hoping to lock them in as friends forever. When sent as a bulletin those stories could reach my entire network totaling well over 1800 channels in all. In some situations I might have posted a reference fact or just stated my opinion on a video share. I've taken the best of the best and could have easily doubled or tripled the size of this book which if successful I will do a part two, or simply write another based on my romantic adventures, hahaha don't ask. If you're wondering am I all that, the answer is yes and a bag of chips too. Hey, if you see any story that touches your heart send me an e-mail heck it might be in my next book. Btw, I regret to inform you that I could not post the names of the replies I got back due to lack of consent and for other legal reasons. Please pardon the language and any spelling errors in those replies. And last but not least my intentions were never to poke fun of anyone other than myself, Thank you, Jimmy

. . . .

Folks I got an interesting story to tell you, I'm an unofficial member of The Polar Bears Club, you know that group of people who every 1st of the new year go swimming in the Coney Island Beach and brave the cold waters ranging from 0 to 15 degrees Fahrenheit or colder. Why do we do it, maybe to prove our manhood/womanhood and it's a part of a tradition here in the borough of Brooklyn, once the home to the famous Brooklyn Dodgers? This year 2010 I plan a different approach, I'm going in with my birthday suit, you heard it right, buck naked. So if you happen to be in the neighborhood drop on by to wish me good luck and for moral support, but be aware no cameras are allowed well at least where I'm at. Hey, maybe you shouldn't come, it won't be a pretty sight especially when I come out of the cold water, and you know parts tend to shrivel up. Any way I'm not going in so don't waste your time coming. I hope not to see you there, and in the meantime enjoy "Coney Island Baby" by The Excellents, ciao, Jimmy.

Hey I was passing by my local pet shop and the sign in the window read "talking dog for sale." Well light bulbs lit up inside my head, I could make a fortune. So I go inside and there at the counter was old man Grady. So nonchalantly I said "so what's up my man" and he said what the heck I wanted. Nothing in particular, just won some lotto money, don't remind me, and was thinking of buying a dog, got anything special. So he jumped up and said well I got one just right for you, meaning me. So where is it, it's in the back. So I strolled to the back and sure as I'm sitting here telling you this story there was this dog sitting at the corner surrounded by all those talking birds. I walked over to it and said tell me something about yourself then it proceeded to say it had worked for the CIA, the FBI and basically was a spy incognito. Then I rushed to the front and asked old man Grady why you selling the dog, "it lies a lot"!!

Hey folks, I once had a similar situation like Roy Hamilton had, she was only trying to play me and use me. And yes she didn't love me, how I know, she ran off with what I thought was my best friend. I wish them all the best. And when she's finished with him I'll even help him dig that ditch. So take it from the love man, that's me, get yourself a woman/man who is true, non-materialistic, and most of all a bundle of joy. That's all I got to say, enjoy the song, "You Can Have Her," a top # twelve hit on the Billboard Charts in 1961 for the incomparable Mr. Roy Hamilton. Thanks, Jimmy

Hey folks, it's "Another Saturday Night" and you know what that means, I'm in an awful way. Why's that, first of all I just got paid and here I am with no one to talk to. I got to find me a woman real quick or I'm gonna burst. That last time I was hooked up on a blind date and you talk ugly, man she looked like the spitting image of Frankenstein. I guess I'll have to rely on that little black book of mine, the one with all the phone #'s. So here goes nothing, innie, minnie, minnie moe let me flip the pages and where it stops that's the girl I'm gonna call. Wow what a coincidence it's Chantilly Lace, darn it, it's always her. How's that, ok, ok I'll tell you how, she's on every page but please don't say a word, or it's gonna ruin my playboy image if anyone should know. See you around, Jimmy and in the meantime let Cat Stevens tell you some more with his cover version of that Sam Cook song "Another Saturday Night."

** Two Love Quotes For The Ladies In My Life **

That includes you too size 7, size 5 1/2, my naughty girl, my pretty girl, my ballerina girl, my wife to be girl, my angel girl, my fortune teller girl, my awesome red head, my Brazilian beauty, my south of the border Mexican senorita, my Irish lass, my British hottie, my Italian stallion senora, my Georgia peach, my Australian fox, my Norwegian belle, my French lover, my Argentine chica, my Texas Bluebell, my Columbian beauty, my cute little Eskimo pie, my Spanish senorita, my Russian babushka, my Polish poni, my Japanese Geisha girl, my sweet fräulien in Munich town, my China doll, and especially you, you know who you are, hahahaha, you!!

1) Two souls with but a single thought, two hearts beating as one!!!
2) My love for you is a journey starting at forever, and ending at never!!!

The comment above prompted a friend to post this remark below. She probably thought I was a player, a big time playboy. You know American humor can be interpreted differently in Latin and European countries and can get me in hot water, hahaha.

What you are so lucky man!!! Wooww, many women in your heart.
Have you had great love?
Have a nice day!

Note: This comment below was sent to my friend of . . . channel trying to bait her into becoming my friend and getting her to open up, enjoy.

Hey . . . , I heard a rumor that you're running away from home to join the circus. You're thinking of becoming a lion tamer. Well I got some good news for you I used to wrestle alligators and I know the in's and out's about ferocious animals. I once killed a rattle snake with my bare hands and teeth. When the little sucker attempted to bite me, I bit first, right in its neck. Well in your interest I could be your manager, and when you go into the cage with the lions I'll be outside with my Colt 45 and protect you. So what do you say, need a good man, that's me? Can I call you partner, partner, Jimmy

(her reply) haha ok! So you're the crazy man with that comment?? :P

Note: Another comment below to have fun with that girl above. She likes me to this day and she taught me some acronyms, god bless her little heart.

Hey . . . you one hottie chickie, yes you are, do you wanna get married, I have ten kids and eight dogs and a truckful of cats. Don't worry you only got to cook for me, I give them the leftovers, love ya, Jimmy

(her reply back) um . . . yeap sure . . . :PP

Folks, my girl just sent me this video to remind me that our love is a nonstop celebration. That girl gives me love 24/7, just before I go off to work, when I come home for lunch, and when I get home from a hard day's night. I mean she rocks my world. Everything you can imagine, that's what she is, makes a grown man cry. Heck I even call in sick just to spend more time with her. Enjoy the song and let the 'fab four' school you some more, thanks Jimmy!!!

The Beatles—Eight Days A Week (# 1 1965)

Folks I got another story to tell you but you ladies better put a knot on your panties first cos that video currently featured on my channel is based on a true story. Yep I used to date the Pointer Sisters, well not at the same time, all four of them, Bonnie included, and if they knew I would be dead meat and persona non grata, comprende. Yeah I would jump for their love. Omg they had me coming and going, hahaha. Need I say more, yeah check out the song and remember me, Mr. Slow Hand.

Pointer Sisters—Jump (For My Love) (# 3 1984)

Folks, here's another incredible story for you. I was driving on the expressway on my way to work this morning when this fire emergency truck cut in front of me almost pushing me off the road. Oh I was fuming mad, about two miles down the road its back doors opened up and out came flying this cooler box. So as I neared the box, about ten feet away, I slowed down and curious me had to see what was inside. So I pushed it to the side of the road and proceeded to open it up. It was a box full of toes all covered with ice, no really, toes. It was probably bound for a skin graft operation or maybe toe transplants, I never heard of that procedure but what do I know. So I whipped out my cell phone and proceeded to call a 'tow truck'. Hey, hope your day was exciting as mine, have a good one, Jimmy

Note: Another prank story, hope you liked it!

Hey folks, I have a story to tell you and I hope you won't be alarmed with what I am about to say. I was on my way to work this morning when I hopped on to a NYC bus, it was crowded as usual but I did manage to find a seat next to this man who was all dressed up and wearing bling bling to the core, you know jewelry and drunk as a skunk. He had rings, watches, bracelets, and chains all over his body. And to top it off he had his arm leaning outside the window ledge trying to look cool. After a few stops the bus proceeded to make a 90 degree turn to the left. As we were doing that a truck was making a 90 degree turn into our lane when they collided and the man's arm was amputated. There was blood and guts all over the place, it was a gruesome sight.
Pt. 1

Pt. 2
The bus driver immediately pulled to the right and had all the passengers including myself wait for the next available bus while he waited for an ambulance to escort the man to the nearest hospital. Two boys who were on the bus located the arm and were trying to take the jewelry off the man's hand. Since they were having trouble they took the whole arm and ran down the road. A cop car shortly made its way to the scene and we informed them of the boys' actions and they gave chase. They apprehended the boys three blocks away and hand cuffed them. We were later informed that they were being charged with 'arm robbery.' Hope your day was exciting as mine, have a good day!!!

Hey folks, how many of you have experienced a broken heart, me, too many times to count. Why last week this girl dumped me, she was everything a man could possibly want, but most of all she was fully loaded. How's that you ask, how does 36, 24, 36 sound to you. I think they even wrote a song about her, "Brick House," by the Commodores. She had one set of headlights and her rear suspension was too much, let's just say it would cause you to take a double take, triple take. So what caused our breakup, she was tired of my low rider and went with a guy who had a brand new little red corvette. So you see she really did me a big favor, proved that she was just a material girl in this material world. Well one day I'm gonna strike it rich and when that day comes I'll be sporting a Lamborghini or a Maserati and that will teach her to mess with me. See you around, love and peace to you all, Jimmy

Commodores—Brick House (# 5 1977)

My Personal Point Of View Hey folks many of my buddies are presently divorced and I noticed they had one thing in common; they all married a pretty woman. Now I have a friend named Popolino who married an ugly chick and they are the only couple still happily married to this day. Popolino figured that if he married an ugly woman he would be happy for the rest of his life. For one thing, she'll always cook his meals and give him peace of mind knowing nobody would hit up on her. They have been happily married now over 30 some odd years. My question to you, would you marry a good looking soul-mate who has the tendency to flirt or would you marry an ugly woman/man. Me personally and I hope you take it from "my personal point of view;" I would look what's in her purse first and then make up my mind. You see my daddy didn't raise me a fool, I'm cool, enjoy the song!!!

Jimmy Soul—If You Wanna Be Happy (# 1 1963)

Note: Jimmy Soul netted this chart topper in 1963 that would cause uproar because the womenfolk felt they were being put down, in either case it was a smash hit!

Hey folks, especially you single ladies out there, yes it's me Jimmy, the 'Handy Man.' I know what you're thinking, what do I do, well for starters I mend broken hearts. How, good question, I whisper sweet nothings into your ears that excites you to no end, need I say more. Just remember, words only for you, and you, and you. Love ya, in the meantime enjoy this song below by that other Jimmy fella, thanks Jimmy

Ps
Tell all your friends, I'm available 24 hours a day, 7 days a week

Jimmy Jones—Handy Man

Note: Jimmy Jones had this # top two hit on the Billboard Charts in 1960 that would become his biggest solo venture. I featured it on my channel and if you get a chance listen to it or better still buy it, you won't be sorry!!!

Hey folks, last year I lost my job due to the recession. Man I was broke, yeah that's right flat busted, no Lincolns, no Georges, or Benjamin's. And to make matters worse my old lady told me to pack my things and go. So I tried working my charms and said "honey you can't mean that, who else is gonna rub your toes when you get home from work, massage you all over." And then she looked me straight in the eyes and said she needed a man with a J. O. B. Well this song will better explain my situation, enjoy, Jimmy!

Ray Charles—Hit The Road Jack (# 1 1961)

Note: Ray Charles netted this # one hit in 1961 on the Billboard Charts and it's true I had a hard time finding a job when I moved back to NY, all the skills I had were useless in an economy that was cutting jobs faster than you could spell JOB

Hey folks, I'm so happy because my girl sends me all kinds of stuff and says I'm her magician, no her Houdini to be exact. Why yesterday she sent me an e-mail while I was at work and the attachment contained a photo of her in her birthday suit, that's right naked as a jay bird. It was just to remind me what I was going to get when I got home, her, and the whole nine yards. Choo, I told my boss I was a little dizzy and if I could be excused and he said why not. So I rushed on home and bought her a bouquet of roses and placed them on our bed. Don't have to tell you the rest other than it was pure heaven, say no more. Enjoy the song "My Baby Must Be A Magician" by The Marvelettes, Jimmy

Note: My comment was based on this top 17 hit song from 1968 by the group above out of the Motown label. Check it out and also these two notable replies I got in response!

Ha! Hey Jimmy thanks for sending me that great Marvelettes story. Score one for the home team! Take care Bro.

Julian

Whoaaaaaaaaaaaaaa Jimmy, I am sure your girl is singing around the room "I am sure my baby is a magician, because he sure has the magic touch" . . . . She is one lucky girl . . . . you better hang on to this one . . . . dance all night long with her . . . . hugssssss . . . L

Hey folks I once had a girlfriend named Marie and every time we went to the dance hop that bone head Billy Joe would try to steal her away from me and put on a big show. He had those fancy moves and would hold her so tight which made me even more jealous. Whenever I tried to cut in he would swift her away and I had to remind him that she belonged to me and that I was taking her home; but somehow I got the impression she forgot I was around. So to get even I did what The Contours did in that song "Do you Love Me," I grabbed Marie and I laid down my dancing moves that not even Billy Joel could keep up, enjoy the two songs below.

The Rocky Fellers—Killer Joe (# 16 1963)
The Contours—Do You Love Me (# 3 1962) (# 11 1988)

Note: The comment above was based on this Rocky Fellers' song. They were a family group consisting of their father and four sons. "Killer Joe" would climb to the 16 spot on the Billboard Charts in 1963 and gain them lots of fame. See this reply below from a dear old friend!

Now Jimmy forget about Marie and come dance with me . . . . We can show Marie and Billy Joel how to cut a rug . . . . LOL . . . . that is if you think you can keep up with my dance moves . . . . LOL . . . . Or you can stand back and watch Marie's mouth drop to the floor . . . . LOL . . . . What are friends for . . . . ? I got your back Jimmy . . . . LOL . . . . Hugs . . . . L . . .

I must thank her for the funny remarks, what a witty gal, and I'm so lucky to have her in my corner, we give each other support when the chips are down!!!

Hey folks, I was thinking about going to that town where the women are not only little, but awesome to say the least, and crazy in a good way. I'm gonna get me one and if I have to commute by train, plane, or even walk there, then that's what I gotta do. So if you don't hear from me any time soon, know where I'm at. Let Wilbert Harrison tell you some more with his chart topper from back in the day, 1959 to be exact called Kansa City, ciao and how, Jimmy

Folks I got a story you just ain't gonna believe, I was involved in a car accident that had my arm barely hanging on a string. The good news was that a lady had just died and they were harvesting all her organs and body parts and they were considering giving me an arm transplant the first of its kind. The only drawback was that it was a lady's and her arm was a lot smoother and hairless, so I went ahead and they performed the 35 hour surgery without a hitch. A few weeks later on a follow up visit the doctor asked me did I have any problems and I said "yes only one, every time I go to pee her hand won't let go," hahaha, enjoy this Roy Hamilton song and do think of me every time you hear "Don't Let Go" ciao, Jimmy

Note: The comment above was to amuse my friends; I think it might have startled a few. The song would reach the thirteen spot on the Billboard Charts in 1958.

Yes folks I too have a cute little girlie on the other side of the tracks in that place they call the "Sugar Shack." I'm not a coffee lover but whenever I want to see that little gal I hop right on over and spend some cash, and talk some trash, and drink it till I can't no more. Hope one day to make that little girl mine, haha, enjoy Jimmy Gilmer he too got's a little girlie of his own right there at the "Sugar Shack," a # one hit for him in 1963, ciao, Jimmy

Enjoy this reply by one of my dear friends.

♥•.*"*•¸•*"*•¸•*"*•❀❤❀•*" *•¸•*"*•¸•*"*•♥
Hellooooo Jimmy . . . Just passing to wish you a great weekend buddy
Ah by the way, about that Sugar Shack . . . If, I was your little girlie in your sugar shack you become a homeless my dear, because I would eat the shack . . . XD LOL
. . . ✯ . . . Have a beautiful day friend . . . *‿*
Much Love for you . . . . *huuuuuuge hug*
♪♫•.*"*•¸•*"*•¸♥

Folks this song by Jeffrey Osborne was a top thirteen hit in 1986 and was one catchy tune that one couldn't resist singing-a-long, well at least I couldn't. Btw can anybody explain what does he mean by "can you woo woo woo." I have no clue as to what he means do you. Well get back to me if you know. Hope you liked it as much as I do, ciao, Jimmy

Jeffrey Osborne—You Should Be Mine (The Woo Woo Song)

Note: Check out this comment below by my good friend in reply to this Jeffrey Osborne song!!

AH AH AH AH LOL LOL LOL
Very funny ""joker""veeeeeery funny indeed XD
I love your sense of humor LOL. Woo Woo Woo XD
. . . ✯ . . . Have a beautiful day Jimmy . . . *‿*
Much Love . . . . *huge hug*
♪♫•.*"*•¸•*"*•¸♥

Hey folks, today I met a hero, I'll tell you something about her. She's pretty, courageous, has a lovely channel, and is downright cool. She has many exploits so let me start by saying she rescued a bunch of kids from a burning building, saved a kid drowning in the river, and rescued a kitten from a high tree. Oh, she's done more than that but she's shy and any more she would be so embarrassed. Let's just say I love her and hope to be her friend forever and a day. By the way her name is Antonija and that's all I'm gonna say other than she's has good choice of music that's out of this world!!!

Note: When I read my friend's profile she stated her occupation as a working class hero. So I made up this story above to brighten up her day and hopefully lock her in as a friend, it worked, we're best of friends to this day. We chat and make goofy comments to each other all the time. See these two replies by her.

I love your channel Jimmy :)

Hey Jimmy, I think we should form a duet we'll be awesome :) hihi and yes of course we are partners ;):)
Thank you for all great videos, I really appreciate it. So, I'll sing and you . . . well you do what you want lol :)
Have a great day . . .

Hey folks I got story to tell you, about ten years ago I had some problems with my baby, so I went to a fortune teller and after reading my palm she said 'Jimmy what you need is a love potion to kick start your mojo'. I yelled out, "what the heck is a mojo." She looked me in the eye and said when you need a little help to arouse your . . . , it's made from an ingredient they make Viagra out of. So I took a squig and said woman are you trying to poison me, it tastes nasty. I stormed out of there upset. When I got home my . . . was stiff as a rock, I proceeded to call my woman and told her I had a present for her so she should hurry right on over. When she walked in I immediately grabbed her and . . . . , and then . . . . , well let's just say our love life has never been the same. And get this I drove her all the way home and that's without leaving the apartment. So if you know anybody having problems tell them to visit that gypsy on 45th and Vine and tell her Jimmy sent you!!!

The Searchers - Love Potion No. Nine (# 3 1965)

Note: Another prank based on The Clovers top 23 hit in 1959. Six years later The Searchers took it to the # three spot on those same charts here in the states.

A lot of people ask me what is my profession. Well prior to writing Rock 'N Roll trivia books I was a professional hit man, yes a killer but I rather not talk about this. I also did time in prison before that for trying to rob a bank and you won't believe this but my grandmother was my getaway driver. We got caught on our first and only robbery attempt; she fell asleep at the wheel. So for any of you thinking of robbing banks get yourself a good getaway driver. I got eleven years and she got two months. She should have gotten those eleven years, heck she's the one who raised me. While in prison I learned the trade very well. I can kill a person with just one bite. I can get out of hand cuffs, use all types of weapons, I'm a master of 3 cards

Monty, and can woo ladies out of all their savings because I'm a lover man, no love girls, not men. So that's it in a nut shell and yes I'm like a squirrel always looking for a nut!!!

Hey folks, I got a story to tell and I hope you don't get insulted, especially if you're a mother or think I'm talking about your mama but what I am about to tell you might upset you. Remember that story about that fortune I won in the lotto. Yeah all $115.93, well that lowdown good for nothing mother-in-law of mine tried to get a piece of the pie as I suspected. Thank the lord she's no longer related to me because her daughter and I are divorced but she's still the grandmother to my kids. She had the audacity to ask me to lend her 85 dollars. She said her cat died and she needed another one or she would have rodent problems. I know what you're going to say, it's an emergency, do it. Heck, she would go out and find a cat in the street or in an alley and then tell me she bought it. You don't know that lady like I know her. She just wants to buy some more wine, Thunderbird or Captain Jack, that old wino. And yes she does look like Satan or his mother because she's one ugly mo-fo. Pardon my French, she just riles me up.
Pt. 1

Pt. 2
When I was dating her daughter back in the day she was so sweet and kind. Yeah, just to butter me up so I would marry her daughter, that cheap so and so. After we got married she was so evil that I never wanted to visit her ever again. When her house burned down she stayed with us for nine months. It was the longest nine months in my life. She's so nosey she had to know everything, like when I got home on paydays, sure as the moon rises; she wanted to know how much I made. Ooohh I just wanted to kill her. The day she left my house I threw the biggest going away party the very same day and we played this song, see the link below. Check it out, I call it "Mother-In-Laws Anthem Song." Hey fellas, do yourself a favor if ever your mother-in-law wishes to move into your home, dig a ditch and throw yourself in it. It will save you the agony. That's all I got to say, Jimmy!

Ernie K-Doe - Mother-In-Law (# 1 1961)

Please note: This prank story above was totally the opposite of what my mother-in-laws were all about. They all loved me like a son and we shared many wonderful times and I have nothing but fond memories of them all.

Folks I got some exciting news to reveal. First of all I've never won a thing in my life, well that goldfish in that little eight ounce bowl doesn't count, plus it died a week later, but don't remind me. You are looking at a lotto winner; you heard it right a winner. I don't know what to do. I got so many things I need so I don't know what I should buy. New converse sneakers are in order, I'm tired of putting cardboard inside the shoe, and it has a hole the size of a half a dollar. Hey, can you give me any suggestions, it's burning a hole in my pocket and I'm not telling any of my friends or family members. If my ex-mother-in-law were to find out she'd be knocking on my doors and windows until I opened up. She's a creature from down under. That's another story I'll tell you some other time. Let's just say she has a spitting resemblance to Satan. So back to me, send me a comment on what I should do with my winnings, all 100 hundred and 15 dollars and 93 cents. Note: This was a prank to make my friends think all I had won was a lousy $115.93 and I'm making a big fuss over it. Well what can I say, I never won anything in my life worth talking about and yes that goldfish doesn't count.

Check out this funny reply below and btw I would have given the whole thing to my mother-in-law if she asked me for it!!!

Hey Jimmy, congratulations on hitting the lotto!!! You the MAN!!!! Sounds like dinner downtown in one of those high class steak or seafood restaurants to me. Thanks for sending me all those great videos. Take care, and have fun with your winnings!

Julian

Second note: Sounds like a diss to me, Julian is just probably jealous that I'm a winner!!!

Hey size 7, you know who you are: Somebody asked me "how long do I plan on keeping you in my life" I smiled and asked how do I choose between always and forever.

Note: Comments like this had everyone wondering what girl I was talking about. In reality it was meant for my friend out west whose shoe size was a 9 not a 7!!!

Hey folks, on a serious note there are three songs that really move me and this one currently playing is one of them. There's nobody out there that has not been affected or been through hard times as a result of drugs, alcohol, or loneliness. Personally I have been spared; but I have friends and relatives who have not. Dion DiMucci, the popular male artist of the late 50s and 60s, you might remember him from his original rendition of "Abraham, Martin And John" song of 1969, sings it so eloquently and I can only imagine what those folks are going through to battle their demons. Please check out this song and you too will be inspired as I am thank you, Jimmy.

Dion - Your Own Back Yard (# 75 1970)

Ps
The other two songs are "Wind Beneath My Wings" the Gary Morris original version and "I Hope You Dance" by Lee Ann Womack. Check out this reply below

Hey Jimmy, thanks for sending me the Dion tune "Your Own Back Yard." Man he tells a powerful story, one that many of us can relate to. Thank God for today, a new day of light . . . out of darkness! Always good to hear from you. I hope that your Mom is on the mend. Stay well and I'll talk to you soon.

Julian

Hey folks, I just wanted to share with you another of my favorite songs that has given me so much joy because it reminds me to never give up in life. Listen to the words and I am sure you too will agree it's a song of hope and inspiration. So when you're feeling low and stress is getting the best of you put on this song and it will inspire you to stand tall and yes even dance because life is worth fighting for. Step up to the plate and go for that brass ring. Enjoy this fabulous song "I Hope You Dance" by Lee Ann Womack. Thank you so much, Jimmy

Lee Ann Womack - I Hope You Dance (# 14 2000)

Hey folks I have a story to tell you, I know you won't believe it, but I see dead people. No, not just any ordinary dead people, people in their birthday suits, yes that's right, naked. I don't know if this is a curse or am I blessed. I'm going to see my fortune teller and see what she thinks. The last time I saw that gypsy woman she tried to set me up on a blind date and that girl was one ugly mo-fo, if you get my drift, must I draw you a picture. She had tattoos all over her body including her butt and had four gold teeth. Ooohh you don't want to know. So what do you suggest I do, go see a shrink or go to my fortune teller? Let me know what you recommend. Thanks, Jimmy

Note: Another crazy story based on that 1999 Bruce Willis and Haley Joel Osment movie 'The Sixth Sense,' hope you like it!!!

Hey folks, it's me again just back from a highly classified undercover assignment. For those of you new to my channel, I'm a retired professional hit man, yes you heard it right, a killer, and still one on rare occasions when called upon, but let's not go there it could put my life in danger. Well I'm back to put a smile on your faces with my awesome collection of rock and roll hits and those love ballads on my theloveman11378 channel and let's not forget jimmyscomedyshop where you can hoot and holler while being entertained with the best comedy sketches that have ever graced the screens, movie and TV. I would like to thank one and all who left me a comment or shared a joke or two and that goes: for Angela, Rita, Tina, and let's not forget my dear old friends Lisa the dancing queen, and Robin, aka Chilliburger, all part of my Mambo # 5 house band. Love you all, big Jim aka The Dancing Machine!!!

Lou Bega - Mambo No. 5 (A Little Bit Of . . .) (# 3 1999)

Note: This song was a # three hit on the Billboard Charts in 1999 by Lou Bega. It helped make the Mambo popular once again and me the Mambo King, don't ask!

This is for all the girls in my life especially you 'brown eyes, it's my number one favorite all-time Motown song charted by The Temptations back in 1965 who were a big part of that huge organization that ruled the airwaves from the 60s into the 80s. Berry Gordy Jr. is no longer the head honcho of that prestigious label but it's still very active today. Thanks and do enjoy this song, my song, "My Girl," Jimmy!!!

A dear friend of mine sent me this reply below after getting my invite to be my friend and I did it by sharing this Temptation song!!!

Yo Jimmy . . . "I've got sunshine on a cloudy day . . ." gr8 channel . . . the music is "FANTASTICO." . . . gotta get back to singing, "talkin about my girl" . . . Thanks for the invite! Peace, . . . =)

Another sweet reply to my Temptation song "My Girl" that I sent to all my friends at that point in time!!!!

> . . . Hi Jimmy . . . Wow! . . . The Temptations . . . just plain beautiful I'm at a loss for words, well, almost! . . . ♫♪,,¬.•*¨I've got sunshine on a cloudy day when it's cold outside, I've got the month of May *•♪♋♪*♪♫

> Hey folks, on Wednesday I had a hernia operation and I'm in a lot of pain. Any wrong movements and I see stars. I walk very slowly, climb steps one at a time, and gently sit down. The good part is that I convinced my doctor to give me a triple. Well since I'm under the knife why not have some cosmetic improvements done. I had a butt transplant, it's like a breast implant except they stuff those little bags in my butt to make me look more muscular and also I had a penis enlargement. Why you ask, some girls like a man with a big d . . . so I had it done. This way when I go to the beach I'll get everyone's attention. Hope you're all happy for me, and don't be jealous, go and have something enlarged yourself, and send me some before and after photos. I'll keep them confidential, for my eyes only!!!

Note: The comment above prompted a friend to send me this reply; she was dead serious about my statement and did not realize I was pulling off another prank.

> Hello there, thanks for droppin' by on my page.
> Well, you have a great page here and I think I have to learn more about romance from you LOL! Anyway you're a funny guy XOXO! But you're too open to say that about the enlargement XD! For me . . . it doesn't really matter if big or small. The most important to me is I love the person.

I sent this e-mail below to a friend cos I had noticed she was not responding to my crazy pranks so to set her straight this is what I told her!!!

> Hey . . . , recently I told you about me having a sex change operation, and about me being in jail, and my cat's pet dying, well they were all fabricated lies intended to make you laugh. You must think I'm crazy if I'm going to stop loving the ladies by having an operation that will end my loving what I love the most, girls, and you included. I made a lot of people laugh but a few of them thought I was for real. What did you think, be honest. Btw, I decided to create a comedy channel and I hope you will send me a few jokes. I don't care if you don't think they're funny send them anyway, like you send me your videos to rate, send me jokes. I sent you an invitation already and I subbed your channel so we can stay in touch. You're one of my better friends but don't tell that to anyone, they might get jealous. Take care and I love you like always, Jimmy

This was her response!!'

> Hey Joker, just stopping by to say "Hello" and thanks so much for your funny highlights on my channel last night . . . lol . . . ! You have made my day, crazy man! You are the best Joker ever ~ what do you take, Jimmy? That's good stuff ~ I want some . . . lol . . . ! But the

idea of a Comedy Channel is not so bad at all, this would come certainly well and I could promise to you, you would completely come on top on my favorite list! Then I pad the ground with soft moss, if you should decide to jump off the roof . . . lol . . . ! . . . Hahaha . . . ! Wish you a fantastic week, take care Jimmy! Good Night and sweet dreams . . . ♥*¨)
,.•´,.•*´¨) ,.*♥¨)
(,.´♥ (,.• . huggies . . .

Here's an e-mail I would send to my friends from time to time whenever I was in the mood for chatting and that was every day, hahahahaha

> Hey . . . just dropping by to say hi and to compliment you on your awesome channel filled with a lot of goodies. I hope you don't mind that I took a few for myself, couldn't resist especially that Don Henley video, terrific. Hey, if you're into love ballads come on over to my romance channel, theloveman11378 and get mesmerized or If that's not your game then visit my new comedy channel, jimmyscomedyshop if you want to play, see you around, Jimmy!!!

This was her reply!!!

> Hi Jimmy . . . thanks for the sweet compliments on my channel . . . :)))) I am happy to share any of the goodies with you . . . . huggs . . .

This comment below was sent to numerous individuals including my friend . . . His replies had me laughing hysterically; hope you'll enjoy it as much as I did.

> <u>Good news but don't tell no one</u>
> Hey . . . , just knocking on your door to say hello, and to tell you that I'm going to have a sex change but keep it to yourself, I don't want all of You Tube friends to know my business. Oh, I'll still be the love man but only you will know I will now be the love woman. Don't try to talk me out of it, I thought about it all night. Why you ask, I think I like ladies boots so how else will I be able to wear them. I don't want people to think I'm coming out of the closet. Heck you thought I was gay, no way Jose. The best part is yet to come, I will now be able to go into the girls locker rooms and see all those gorgeous bodies in their birthday suits. And you thought I was dumb. Brighter than a light bulb, that's me. So what do you think of me now!!! Jimmy
>
> Ps
> Don't forget mums the word, sssssshhhhh!! Dumb question, you got any ladies boots for sale!

His first reply to me

> Re: good news but don't tell no one
>
> Dakota Jane -
> That's some crazy shit you laid on me. So I take it that you're not a religious man! Since you chose me among all the rest to confide in - at least please tell me where the money's

coming from. Six months ago, you wanted to sell your valuable record collection for some dough during a rough spell. Now you're spending hard-earned dollars on a new pussy! Put down the bottle and make yourself some fucking scrambled eggs!
You thought about it all night? Wow. That's a considerable amount of time to make such a distinct life change. Why not do the Ed Wood thing? Wear your Nancy Sinatra boots and mini at home. But don't get rid of your dick though. You'll miss it.
My first reply to him!!!

Re: Re: good news but don't tell no one

Oh I'm laughing my ass off, you're the 2nd of 3 who I fooled, I sent this to about 30 friends I just can't wait for the others to come in.
    I'm sorry . . . . it was all a joke, I've done 32 pranks in the past 7 days and I'm laughing so hard, you have no idea,

                                                                                    Jimmy

I post them on the comment page so all people can see it and think I'm crazy and then that's when I laugh the hardest!!!

You didn't have your comment set up so I thought I would get half a joke but seeing you mad I'm laughing to no end . . .

His second reply to me

Re: Re: Re: good news but don't tell no one

You dildo, you tested my forbearance. Part of me wanted to pray for you and another part of me wanted to see a picture of your new tits. Anyway, you got my attention. I guess I'll have to be a better friend and check in on your superb channel more often. I'm sorry I haven't done that Fuckhead.

                                                                                    Best

My comment back to him!!

Re: Re: good news but don't tell no one

Hey do me a favor repeat your comment on my channel. I'll have so many others laughing. Please, see what another girl wrote on my channel, she caught on, unlike you, but I know you meant well with that nasty reply, I just love it!!!!!!!!!!

His reply back to me!!!

Re: went off smoothly

All you could think about was her peaches! You should have lifted up your skirt and said ain't that a peach?

This e-mail was also sent to my girl 'friend' . . . who responded back, also funny.

'Hi Jimmy - one question, are YOU HIGH??? And what the H--l are you smoking??? I want some too!!!

I am laughing so hard, I woke up a few people in the house, what kind of message did you leave me??

Oh, by the way, I have plenty of boots, love them. If they fit YOU, they are yours. And I have plenty of other "Stuff" you might like, how 'bout a couple of guys. Since you are going through a change Lol, you can use plenty of what I got, and I got plenty, in fact too much!!!

Omg, you are one funny Dude, love you, thanks for making me howl with laughter . . .
Oh, good luck with your surgery- Ouchhhh!!!

I have a nice Red leather jacket to go with those boots, lol, you will need them to kick some serious butt, cause all the chicks will be after you for stealing their fellas, you said, you arc big and bad right?? I can't stop laughing . . . you are a hoot-
Much Love to You, Jim, honestly - you are crazy, and I like it-

Best to you, hugs, . . . ****** xxx

My 3rd and 4th replies from two of my other friends also funny

Hi Jimmy, I can't help you out on the clothes front: but it looks like you have a big fan base: should be no problem for you. Take it easy and thanks for the laugh. Too little of it around nowadays. Careful with those stilettos!! . . .

Hey Jimmy, is this some kind of a joke you posted on my channel? . . . I can't stop people from seeing it unless I remove it . . . So tell me, what's the real deal, did you spam your own comment on here as well??

Yeah, I figured it was a joke!!! HAHAHAHAHAHAHAHA, yeah, the jokes on me!!!!! I haven't been on lately!!! Take care my friend!!!!

Note: I call this part two of my gender change prank below, went off smoothly.

Hey folks got some good news; remember that sex change operation, well it went off smoothly. Put it this way I have no cajones, for those of you who don't understand Greek, French, or Spanish, no more b . . . s and what used to hang with it. I am now a proud owner of a lovely v . . . . a and hairless at that, which I find cute and plan to keep it like that, hairless. Now I didn't want to tell you this but since the cats out of the bag, no pun intended, I also had a boob job. I am now the proud owner of size 36D. You know that song "Brick House," well I'm now a hot 36, 24, 36, oooh what a winning hand. I had a touché job too, you know it's like a boob job but instead they insert them there bags in the butt, both cheeks. I mean a girl's butt has to have more meat on it and in order to look genuine I had electrolysis work to remove unwanted hair. This morning I went to the gym and met some girls and we shared a sauna
Pt. 1

Pt. 2

It was like heaven all of us chatting and sharing stories naked as a bird. They talked about guys that I found boring and I asked if anybody had a recipe for peach pie. So this one girl, Veronica, came right up to me wearing nothing at all and gave me her formula and all I could think about was her peaches and her . . . Well anyway, we became good friends and plan to meet every week. Later I went to try on some boots and other clothing and when I came out wearing a mini skirt the girls in the room were all in awe, their mouths and eyes wide open I guess when you look drop dead gorgeous, thank you, then you are just that, drop dead gorgeous. I then rushed over to have a pedicure and my eyebrows waxed. You know I got to keep my gorgeous look especially with these new pair of boots I bought at Lord & Taylor's, only the best for the best. Well I gotta go, see ya, hate to be ya. Love, Dakota Jane f/k/a Dakota Jim

Check out these two replies!!!

Oh Jimmy . . . so lovely to hear you are so well after your big operation *smiles* . . . I am really happy for you. Just imagine all the good times you are going to have with your new girlfriends . . . coffee shopping . . . Omg!! Are you going to share your new recipe with your friends here??? I am so jealous you have new boots. Might have to go shopping myself. Wanna come?? . . . Well you enjoy your new "freedom" and don't forget to drop in and say hello every now and then . . . Luv & {hugs} xxx

hahaha . . . Jimmy you are a nutter!!!

Here's a reply from another friend!!!

Jane, puleeeze! Have a great weekend and thanks for the laughs! xoxo, ...

Folks, I sent a few of you funny anecdotes, please don't take them seriously. They are only to put a smile on your face and maybe a chuckle. So if you are one of the lucky ones, please enjoy, Jimmy

Note: This remark above I posted on my page because some people were starting to believe I was one sick puppy, having a gender change and so forth. I had to set them straight, yes, that I was a straight man!!!

Here's an e-mail I sent to a friend!!!

Hey . . . , I was wondering since we are two hot chicks, maybe we can get together and paint each other's toe nails and then paint up the town. If you like we can go to the gym, I know one that has a sauna room, you know it's good for the complexion and we can talk recipes, girls, and recipes, and girls, and girls. Are you down, pick you up in 15 minutes, here's your hat, what's your hurry!!!

A lady liked my channel so much she sent me this reply with her invitation to be her friend and French games ooooh la la what can I lose hahahahahaha!!!

Can I order a daily message from you? I would like that very much. I need, like everyone else, the laughter and the adventure. Can I come over so we can play? I know French games . . . you probably have never played before :) Love, . . .

Hey folks I just got rejected by a lady somewhere out west, when I asked her to be my friend, I think her name was Angel, she made me feel so bad that now I have to tell you some awful news. My real name is not Jimmy, its JJ, but my best friends call me Jocko. I was just released last month from the penitentiary after doing eleven years of hard time. I used to rob banks and on my first attempt I got caught. Why you ask, where else in America can a poor boy like me become an instant millionaire overnight, in reality in ten minutes if it's done right. Well I got caught, do yourself a favor never have your grandmother as your getaway driver. The damn fool fell asleep at the wheel and here I am telling you this horror story. She did two months' time and me eleven years. Let me learn you some, if for any reason you end up in the pokey, that's what we call the jail, Pt. 1

Pt. 2
make sure that on your first visit walk in like you just killed 19 or 26 people bare handed, and have a cocky walk like don't f . . .k with me, I'm bad, kind of attitude. Well that's what I did and every now and then give a hoot. Man they won't dare mess with you, and dig this, disguise your voice and talk dirty and curse like the best of them. Shake no hands, take no prisoners, and everything will work out wonderfully. I know I'm a living proof. When you eat, don't use a fork chew your meat like you want to eat somebody's heart out and I'll tell you they will move away from you, even the big guys won't dare mess with you. Tell them you were an eight time Kung Foo champion and that you taught Brucie all he knew. Bruce Lee, who else did you think I was referring too? Hey, one last tip, don't bathe; they'll surely stay away from you then. Please keep this to yourself, I shine shoes at the corner, if anybody finds out I might get booted off their blocks. C ya!!

Hey Folks, for your information, three girls thought I was referring to them, one because her name was Angel. A gentleman never tells, hahahahaha!!!

Folks, I got some bad news to tell you, this morning one of our pets died, I don't know how to break it to our other pet. I'll probably be out of the office for a week or two in mourning. Let me start all over, we have a cat by the name of Goldie and my daughter bought Goldie her very own pet. I know what you're thinking; one pet is as good as another, and what the heck is a pet having a pet. Well for those of you who aren't too bright it happens all the time. Why not less than five days ago we were watching an animal documentary on The Discovery Channel, or was it Wild Kingdom. It had to be Wild Kingdom, we don't subscribe to The Discovery Channel. In the documentary they presented this gorilla, Tequanda or Quanda, with a kitten for its birthday. Now you would think no way Jose, yes way it really happened.
Pt. 1

Pt. 2

You would think the gorilla would pull the kittens legs right out of its socket. Well to our surprise she cuddles it all day long and ever so gently. And that ape won't allow any of her kids, baby gorillas, near the poor thing. So that proves it's possible for a pet to own a pet. Any way Goldie loved her pet, she would chase it all day long, smother it, and always trying to smack it. My daughter named it Flippa. So this morning I found Flippa face down in the top of the pool. So I was wondering folks what should I do. I was thinking to myself, self maybe I should run over to the 99 cents store before anybody wakes up and buy another goldfish. Yeah good idea, then I can flush the dead one down the toilet and the matter solved. Why didn't I think of that in the first place? Folks we have a correction Jimmy, me, won't be out of the office after all. We're back to normal. Thanks just the same and have a wonderful day, love you all, Jimmy

Note: Another prank story, people probably thought I was insane making a big deal out of a dead gold fish. Hey, it would break a child's heart if his or her gold fish died.

theloveman11378

THE ROMANCE CHANNEL

SUBSCRIBE

Folks when I was a kid of seventeen I was seduced by a woman nearly twice my age, she was so infatuated with me but I did not see it coming She asked me to come over to her house to do a paint job and to get there after midnight. Why so late, it didn't dawn on me but as we were removing all the furniture she saved the bed for last and that too kind of surprised me. Then she brought me a plateful of exotic foods, clams, mussels, shrimp, and crab meat; she said I deserved a bonus. Then she brought in two glasses and a bottle of red wine and put on the stereo and had The Delfonics singing all their greatest hits. Woo I love The Delfonics, and as we chatted she kept pouring me more and more wine. Shortly after I was starting to feel a bit woosey so I had to lay down a bit, and before I knew it she came into the room buck naked. Omg I then realized what she was up too, but I was helpless as a kitten and she had her way with me. Moral of the story, never work after midnight hahaha, enjoy The Delfonics, ciao, Jimmy

The Delfonics—Didn't I (Blow Your Mind This Time) (# 10 1971)

Folks, I got myself in a jam, let me explain. Yesterday I was strolling with my girl, yeah the one that rocks my world, and as I was about to give her a kiss I could see the glee in her eye. So I says to her "what is it that you want, you want the moon well I'll lasso it for you" and she cocked her head up to the sky and responded she'll take it. What am I going to do now? Well this weekend I'll take her to the beach late at night, hire a waiter to serve us champaign and play moon songs

Jimmy Stewart—Lasso The Moon (It's A Wonderful Life) (1946)

Folks that's the late great Billy Stewart with one of his unforgettable love ballads currently featured on my channel. I'm gonna tell you an interesting story how he came up the ranks. It is rumored he entered a talent show and when it was his turn to sing everybody in the audience began to laugh at him cos he was wearing a big ole hand-me-down suit probably his daddy's. But the minute he started to sing he had the audience melting in the palm of his hands; needless to say he won that night. We lost him in 1970 way too soon from a car accident, he may be gone but not his legacy. They should make a movie based on his life story to inspire others who may or may not be as talented but to know there is hope out there, ciao Jimmy

Billy Stewart—I Do Love You (1965)

27

Folks when you have the two most important key ingredients to a romantic love scene, a song to die for, and two sexy lovers in a warm embrace getting ready for that final act of love making what else can you say. Well for me this is my favorite hottest movie love scene of all time; it's from the movie 'Ghosts' but then that's my opinion. What say you out there in YT land which one is yours? Send it to me right here and I'll feature it on this channel with your name or if you want to remain anonymous well that's your choice too, ciao Jimmy

Ps
All of a sudden I have this urge to wanna make pottery, can you blame me, hahahaha
Unchained Melody—Ghost (Love Scene) (1990)

Folks when the British Invasion was at its peak here in the states during the 60s The Walker Brothers did the reverse, they went over there to the UK and made a huge impact and a big name for themselves. This song currently featured on my channel, "Make It Easy On Yourself" was a remake of a Jerry Butler top 20 hit song from 1962 and they took it four notches better at the 16 level in 1965. Both are well done, enjoy The Walker Brothers version, ciao Jimmy

Folks I got a story you're just not gonna believe, you know when you love somebody so much and you can't let go. No what I mean you really can't let go. Well I've come up with a solution, I'm gonna write up a prenuptial agreement with my woman that if either one of us should die well that's not the end of the world. We'll go to a taxidermist and have the body stuff and mounted. Hahahaha, I told you wouldn't believe it. See this way when the survivor, me or her, gets that urge, you know what I'm talking about, must I draw you a picture. Well you climb up on that ladder and hop on hahaha, yes go have your way with her/me. Wow, what a great idea, so what do you think, did I come up with a winner, let me know, and yes "Please Don't Go," enjoy KC And The Sunshine Band, he's the one who gave me this idea, well not exactly but through his song. Ciao and how Jimmy!!!

Folks I just love this song by Skeeter Davis and yes she and I have so much in common so I'm gonna ask you a question, if the world did come to an end today what would you do. Well I would come over and rock you one more time for the good times. And like they do on an airplane, put my head between my legs and if we were to crash I would be able to kiss my ass goodbye, hahaha. Enjoy Skeeter Davis, it is the ultimate sad song I have ever heard, just the thought of losing you would have one devastating effect on me that it would be my end of the world too, ciao, Jimmy
Skeeter Davis—The End Of The World (# 2 1963)

Folks I got a story to tell you that you just might not believe and for you ladies out there you might have to tie a knot on your bloomers. I'm really a midget, we don't like to be called that, we prefer small people, no different than you or your kids. God created all types of people and we are proud, we're invincible, and if you ever see me walking down the street, call me Jimmy or Jockomo, my wrestling nickname, but never midget cos then I'll have to body slam you and hurt you. Hey, enjoy Randy Newman, that big jerk,

Randy Newman—Short People (# 2 1978)

No that's not me taking a shower, but I sure wish it was, he had them girls all excited and you just know I can bump with the best, so if bumping is your game, call me hahahaha love to bump. Shooo I was bumped up ahead of the class cos I brought the teacher an apple and she now calls me her boy lollipop. Hey if that will get me an "A" then I can be anything you want me to be, your poppie, your sugar daddy, wooo say no more, byeeeeee Jimmy

Banned Axe Commercial—Shower Girls

Folks I got a story you're just not gonna believe, this summer I am going to hit all the beaches dressed like that, yep wearing a bikini. And I don't mean just any polkadot bikini, one with a thong, so when I stroll up and down the sandy shore gonna get me a full body tan. See if you walk you get a full sun covering and I will look hot. I was thinking instead of yellow how about hot pink, hey maybe you wanna come with me; yeah we can talk about anything, boots, halters, silk underwear. Yeah I got all those things so I hope to see you around and please don't be jealous cos you too can wear a drop dead gorgeous bikini if you got the cajones hahaha, enjoy the video, Jimmy

Hey, you see those two girls laughing, they were just jealous. I met them in the locker room and may I say they are hot, like me, bye bye . . .

Just For Laughs—Bikini Man

Hey, I went on a date with a girl who looked a lot like Wanda, she tried to pick me up, no not that way, lift me in her arms like a cave man would to a cave woman. She almost broke my hip when we were dancing, and she wanted me to have a night cap at her house, well don't remind me, enjoy 'In Living Color,' ciao Jimmy

Wanda's Blind Date—from the TV show 'In Living Color'

Folks, I went to see my doctor the other day cos I had some symptoms that I needed evaluated. So I told him what I had, my heart beating abnormally, it keeps going pada boom, pada bing, a funny sensation in my belly, a shortness of breath, walking in a daze, weak at my knees, and unable to sleep as a result of my tossing and turning. Then he says, hmmm not good, not good at all. He places a stethoscope on my chest and I can hear him muttering something or other. He takes his gavel to test my knee reflexes and then he checks my mouth and my ears. Feeling concerned my hands begin to tremble expecting the worse. He says I got some good news and some bad news. The good news, my findings is that you're in love. In love, hey is that what all these signs point to. Yes, and for the bad news, there's no cure for what you got. Then I get up and give him a great big hug. What's that for? For making my day, gonna go see my girl and make love to her. See ya and do enjoy Elvis, ciao Jimmy

Elvis—All Shook Up (# 1 1957)

29

Folks ever hear the expression getting pissed off, well this blind guy is doing just that, he's peeing on people as they are boating in a little lake and as a matter of fact they aren't too happy, they are pissed off, hahaha. Check it out you too will pee in your pants or draws from laughing so hard, ciao, Jimmy

Just For Laughs—Guy Peeing on People in a Lazy River

Folks I need your opinion on something, I just met a woman, is it proper to ask her to let me paint her toe nails, and then I let her paint my toe nails, and then we go out and paint up the town? Why, cos I am smitten by her, she's got the prettiest eyes and when she walks she wiggles, and when she talks giggles that just drive me wild. Oh, what am I to do, so that's why I ask you for your advice, thanks Jimmy

Ps
She calls me 'Baby Boy' and I call her 'Baby Girl'

DJ Boonie—Baby Boy

Folks that's another of my favorite comedy movies, if you haven't seen "Home Alone (Parts 1 & 2)" you don't realize what you're missing, they are the bomb, Joe Pesci steals the show every time. Go out and rent them or better still buy them to add to your collection you won't be sorry, ciao Jimmy

Home Alone (Parts 1 & 2)—Booby Trap Montage!

Folks there are many great movies and this scene from, 'Planes, Trains, & Automobiles' is definitely one of my favorites of them all. Those two knuckle heads, Steve Martin & John Candy, are the reincarnation of Laurel & Hardy, so sit back and watch it from its entirety and be prepared to cry laughing, hahaha, Jimmy

Planes, Trains, & Automobiles—(highway scene 2)

Folks today while visiting a friend of mine I came across this lovely song on her channel that melted me in such a way that I just had to share it with you. Reading the song comments I see many people also like it and some even want it to be played for when they die. Not me I want it for me now, it's for the living, dead won't do a thing for me, so please check it out, it's a gem, a keeper, ciao, Jimmy

No Mercy—When I Die (1997)

Folks I got a "Calendar Girl" of my own, haha, she's got a touch of everything a man could possibly want in a woman. She's pretty, sweet, witty, caring, giving, and a bit naughty. Why she came to my house the other day in a trench coach and when she walked inside and took it off, omg you don't want to know. She didn't have a stitch of clothing on other than her boots and may I say they were somethng else them boots. I marched her straight into the bed room and you don't need for me to tell you what happened next. Ok, ok she jumped on me and we didn't stop till the milkman rang the bell the next morning. Wooo that was one heck of a party and tomorrow we're gonna do it again. Maybe I'll come over to her house wearing a trench coat and boots, she lent me hers' hahaha, good bye gotta call her and thank her for one swell time, ciao and how, Jimmy

30

Ps
Enjoy Neil Sedaka with "Calendar Girl" a top # four hit on the Billboard Charts in 1961

Folks I'm a gun for hire, you got a boyfriend, a husband, a girlfriend, a wife, a boss, a lawyer, a doctor, a mother-in-law you want out of your misery well I'm your man. And I don't come cheap, it's 150 smakeroos, no not dollars, 150 thousand dollars is more like it, USD not in Yens or Pesos. Well I do a good job, you won't be incriminated, and I do it quick and easy. So tell me how do you want it done, painlessly, like in an explosion or do you want them to suffer pain, like ripping their nails off their bodies first or feeding them to the crockadiles, let let me know you know where to find me, at theloveman11378 24/7 and it's all cash no IOU's, ciao. Jimmy

Ps
Starting today call me Kemosabe and yours will be Tonto, and enjoy Leonard Cohen cos like me, he's your man . . .

Leonard Cohen—I'm Your Man (1988)

Hey folks I can't understand for the love of me why my grandmother would want to set your grandmother's flag on fire and why the heck Captain Jack wants off that island. Shoo if it were me I would put on a grass skirt and party with them native girls till I can't no more. And talk about coconuts, I would love to drink some all day long, builds strong bones if you get my drift, hahahaha, enjoy Iko Iko, ciao Jimmy

Captain Jack—Iko Iko (1995)

Folks John Wayne, America's greatest action hero, is rumored to have been partially responsible for two things, this song featured on my channel is one of them. How's that, well when Buddy Holly was writing this song he was stuck with the lyrics and while watching the movie 'The Searchers' he took John's words from a scene and incorporated it into the song, "That'll Be The Day." What's the other thing, John would say "Corky we're saddling up we're going south to please Missy." Now you know why you girls get so excited when us guys say those words, it's gonna be one heck of a ride, hahaha, enjoy the song and don't mind me, Jimmy

Yes folks that's me to a 't' single and free and if you want some it's yours for the taking, cos I will more than tickle your fancy. Wanna know more, experience is what I am, so if you got what I don't then call me and bring me some sugar and while we're at it lots of spending loot will also do the trick. Did I say trick, girl I will give you lots of tricks and treats and it ain't even Halloween? What is it that you want me to do, hey this is a family show don't be talking nasty, but I can get good and nasty as you want me to get, hahaha. You see I've been around the block more times than you can count, shoo the last time I had a fling with a gal I think she's still in never never land and doesn't wanna come down, so check me out, and also The Honey Cone, ciao and how, Jimmy, aka the love man

Honey Cone—Want Ads (# 1 1971)

31

Folks I got something personal to tell ya, I love that pussy of mine and she knows it but it always plays the field, hard to get is more like it. I literally worship the ground she walks on and I let it out at night to roam the streets. But I still can't make her love me. You see, Bonnie Raitt and I are in the same predicament and sometimes I just wanna die cos I need it so bad, I'm ready to explode. I can't sleep without it, I think of it day and night. I sometimes climb the walls looking for it. Last night it jumped right on my face I almost choked to death. I really think she's got a craving for that tom cat outside. Well maybe she deserves a treat heck she rids me of mice and is the best bug repellent ever. So yes I'm gonna let Pookie, that's my cat's nickname, go out but let me put out a fresh bowl of milk and kitty treats first. Thanks for listening, ciao, Jimmy

Bonnie Raitt—I Can't Make You Love Me (1992)

Hey this question is for the ladies out there, have you ever had a spat with your lover boy and then you realized you were wrong. Well that's what happened to me and she tried every trick in the book from sending me flowers, a bottle of the finest wine, a cologne all with intents to reconcile but what really did the trick was when she came over all wrapped up in her trench coat and when she came inside the door and took it off she didn't have a stitch of clothing underneath. Oh lordie lord, good god in heaven is this woman sweet, how I know, I had a mouthful hahaha don't ask I said a mouthful already. Enjoy The Equals with "Baby, Come Back" a # 32 hit in 1968, bye bye . . . . Jimmy

Folks I got some good news and some bad news to tell you. First the bad news I went to see my fortune teller to have her read my fortune and after paying her the usual donation, that's what she calls it to avoid paying taxes, she proceeded to take out that bowling ball that she calls her crystal ball and as she started to stare at it she began to cry uncontrollably. Omg then I joined in and started to cry and she gave me a dirty look and told me my gal had run off with a clown from the circus. I was so depressed but here's the good news as I was walking out I bumped into the most gorgeous girl I have ever seen and she gave me a wink. Oooo la la my lonely days are over, tell you some more some other time, but in the meantime enjoy Lou Christie, ciao Jimmy

Lou Christie—The Gypsy Cried (1963)

Folks I don't know about you but when I'm not with my gal I sometimes get to wondering what she's doing tonight. Is she cooking up a storm, writing me a love letter, or polishing her toe nails without me cos that's something I like doing painting her toe nails so she can then do mine so then we can paint up the town afterwards. Oh we're crazy like that you don't wanna know the silly stuff we do. Why the other day I jumped over this lady's fence and picked three dozen of her roses. I picked so many the poor lady would have had the right to shoot me, and another time we both jumped into a neighbors pool buck naked we didn't make any noise just stood there holding each other and, and well you can only imagine. Byeeeee, and do enjoy Boyce & Hart they too are wondering, no not about us, some gal of theirs hahaha, Jimmy

Tommy Boyce & Bobby Hart—I Wonder What She's Doing Tonight (# 8 1968)

Folks I got a story to tell you that you just ain't gonna believe, do you know what Mickey & Minnie, Romeo & Juliet, Samson & Delilah have in common with me and my lady love, well when we get to making love it's like a five alarm fire cos we are so hot something's bound to give. Omg you can fuhgettaboudit cos nothing is gonna cool us down no how. You know what they say, you fight fire with fire, but then that's another story for another day in the meantime enjoy the Pointer Sisters who will tell you some more, ciao, Jimmy

Pointer Sisters—Fire (# 2 1979)

Folks I got another story to tell you, when I was a little kid I would play with Pookie Girl and I just loved to play Cowboys & Indians and heroes & villains. Pookie on the other hand would always get mad cos she was always the Indian or the villain. She had other plans like playing mom & dad. Well now that we've grown up I wanna play Mr. & Mrs. cos then she allows me to tie her up and do all those crazy things grownups like to do, yep chain her to the bed, etc. etc. hahaha, enjoy Peaches & Herb, ciao, Jimmy

Peaches & Herb—Two Little Kids (1967)

Folks I've compiled a comedy playlist of all the greatest comedy scenes and commercials. It will have you laughing so hard you might end up crying or peeing on yourself. Come to my channel and copy any or all and I like to wish you or yours a Happy Father's Day, Jimmy

Folks here's another of my favorite comedy scenes from my "Jimmy's Comedy Playlist.". Well I just love Mrs. Brown, well not the way you think, for anybody who is not familiar with Mrs. Brown she's not really a woman, so I wouldn't be caught dead making love to Mrs. Brown she's a man under all that disguise, and I am a straight man. I love what you girls have that I don't have hahahaha, hope I didn't lose you, and if you need further interpretation send me an e-mail if you want me to set you straight. What, I lost you when I made that left turn two blocks down, hahaha, enjoy and get ready cos today I will be featuring my movies playlist consisting of all the great movie scenes that will knock your socks off, ciao Jimmy

Mrs. Brown's Bikini Wax—Episode 3—BBC

Yes folks you're hearing this right, Frank Rizzo calls up the Cremation Services so they can melt down his mother and father for the insurance monies, why wait till they die. Not a bad idea, why didn't I think of this brilliant plan myself, maybe you should do the same and remember who gave you the idea, so a tip is appreciated, how about 50%, why 50%, who gave you the idea, so 50% is my cut hahaha. Enjoy The Jerky Boys and don't be surprised if I call you up with another of my great ideas . . . .

The Jerky Boys—Cremation Services

You know someone once asked me to describe myself, sure why not, well besides being handsome, you can see my picture at the bottom of my page, well that's not me but my twin brother, I am sophisticated, intelligent, funny, a Don Juan, an athlete,

33

I can sing and dance like Michael, they say I sound like a cross between Al Green, Freddie Jackson, and Michael Bolton and last but not least make love like a beast. Yep that's me alright and the proof of the pudding I've been around the blocks thirteen times. But if you don't count the three times I was married to one gal, yep she was my shrink then it's eleven in all. Talk about crazy that woman was crazier than me but I guess when you got it like I got it then I'm just a hunk waiting to happen. See you around and if you want a piece of me you know where to find me, right here 24/7, eight days a week, if I'm not home leave me a message and your photo, ciao, Jimmy

Folks I always said what two consenting adults do is no one's business but their own. But in all respect to that chap kissing that mannequin does it pertain to him too. Hmmmmm I wonder, gonna need somebody with legal advice to determine if that chap is out of his rocker and belongs in a mental institution with bars on them cos he may be dangerous to himself, others, or even mannequins. Oh well 'se la vie' is what I also always say, what say you out there in You Tube land, ciao, Jimmy

Just For Laughs—Man Kisses Mannequin

Folks I got to tell you something that happened to me recently that will either inspire you or make you sick, I took my girl to a fancy restaurant and as we were eating she noticed a roach stuck to an ice cube in her drink and she almost fainted and when I pointed it out to the waiter he immediately reported it to the owner of the establishment who told us the dinner and any more drinks was on him and that we could come again for another dinner any time soon. So what do you think, well for me I'm gonna put an ad in the papers asking folks to collect some roaches dead or alive and I'll go to the finest restaurants and do it again and again. Well I will be partying and eating like a rock star that I am hahaha, hey keep this to yourself don't need anyone to ruin this game plan of mine hahaha. I will be putting on weight galore; my 155 pound frame will turn into a massive 225 pounder in no time. Hey maybe you want to give it a try you might just like it, ciao Jimmy

Newbeats—Bread And Butter (# 2 1964)

Folks I got some bad news and some good news to tell you. Remember that incident when Pookie and I went to the restaurant and we found a roach attached to an ice cube in her drink and how all the charges were dismissed and they gave us another free dinner on them to boot. Well here's the good news for the past three days we've been eating at some of the finest restaurants in NYC, breakfast, lunch, and dinners and drinking Dom Pérignon. How did we do it, sshhhh we brought along our own roaches hahaha. Oh I don't have any at home I paid a fella five dollars to bring me some for his troubles. Now here's the bad news I took a bunch of us to an Italian restaurant and when I confronted the waiter with the roach in Pookie's drink he immediately called the owner who upon hearing my complaint grabbed me by the collar and said I would be dead meat if I didn't pay up roaches or no roaches. Pt. 1

Pt. 2

Well lucky for me a cop passing by saw us scuffling and took me in to the courthouse where the judge hearing what had occurred ruled that I had to pay or work it off. Well since my books aren't selling to well lately I took the work detail offer. I have to wash dishes, and pots and pans every weekend for Mr. Don Corleone for the next 6 months or he would make me an offer I couldn't refuse, no not the judge Mr. Don Corleone. Hey how was I to know the late Godfather had a grandson. Oh well my scam was good till it lasted. Moral of the story, don't fecking mess with the mob, roaches or no roaches. Enjoy the movie clip, ciao Jimmy

Marlon Brando—God Father
(I'm Gonna Make Him an Offer He Can't Refuse) (1972)

Folks I got another story to tell you, you remember when I was scamming restaurants for a free meal by planting roaches in the food they wore serving us well I got away with it 25 times but here's what happened on my 26th attempt. I took Pookie and four of our best friends to a fancy restaurant in NYC. Well we ordered the best and two bottles of Dom Pérignon. Oh we were having a swell time, dancing, eating, drinking, and laughing when all of a sudden the roaches in that match box came lose in my suit jacket, all twelve of them as I was dancing. Them critters were crawling all over me and I was itching uncontrollably and started to dance the jitterbug in hopes they would all come out. The folks at the tables were starting to clap for me, I guess I was dancing up a storm and they thought I must have been Fred Astaire reincarnated. Pt. 1

Pt. 2

Pookie looking so surprised and unable to catch up with me looked so happy for me but when I whispered in her ear about the roaches she jumped back and started to laugh uncontrollably but from a distance. Then I noticed the roaches were falling to the ground so I did my Sammy Davis Jr. tap dance routine only to stomp them critters to death. I was smoking hot with my tap dancing and I did manage to kill all but one. When the owner heard and saw my performance and the folks clapping and giving me a standing ovation he took the bill and tore it up and said I should come again. Well I did achieve my goal, a free meal. Well the moral of the story let Pookie hold the roaches and two or three roaches should be more than enough a dozen is way too much, enjoy this Leo Sayer song, he too knows how to get a meal for free, hahahaha ciao Jimmy

Leo Sayer—Long Tall Glasses (I Can Dance) (1975)

Folks I got a story to tell you about my very first encounter with the law, and it's all on account of me wanting to get a screw. Let me start from the beginning. I'm a dabbler, I dabble a bit here and a bit there, no, not the stock market, are you crazy. I just like to tinkle, you know open up things and probe with my hands and eyes. I was having trouble with my tellie, what's a tellie, that's what the folks from the UK call a TV, I see you haven't seen any of those British shows, Mrs. Brown or Sherlock Holmes; they use that word all the time. Back then TV's consisted of tubes, nuts, bolts, and screws so by dabbling I was able to get it going like brand new except I

35

needed a screw or two. So I ran to the mall and I bumped into this dapper looking fellow and I asked him if he knew where I could get a screw, he says at the penthouse at the top of the mall. I not realizing what he meant I work my way to the elevator and the elevator man asks me what floor, to the penthouse,
Pt. 1

Pt. 2
Then he says are you sure and I say where else can I get screw so then he says you've come to the right place. So we reach the top and this palooka looking thug greets me and asks me what I wanted so I say a screw or two. Then he asks me, the 200 hundred dollar model, no, then he says the 150 dollar one and I say no, then he says the 50 dollar piece, and I say no no that's still too high. So he asks me, well how much are you willing to spend, two cents then with a smirk on his face he opens up a door and yells out hey Mac bring up the old cat. Just as he utters those words in rush 25 S.W.A.T. cops and they tell us we're all under arrest for prostitution and before I could say another word they chain us up together and bring us to a paddy wagon and drive us to the courthouse. Sixteen half-dressed girls, two goons, and this well dressed dude who looked like a lady who I surmised was the ring leader. By this time I'm pleading with the lieutenant that I was only looking for a screw then he says that's why you're here. So we're all thrown into a big holding cell with a bunch of other low lifers, mother rapers, father rapers, pick pocketers,

Pt. 3
and god knows what else. So here I am innocent mingling with a bunch of crooks. A few of the girls take notice of me and start winking and showing me their boobs, but by this time all I had on my mind was how was I going to get out of there. When it was my turn to make that one call I called my mama and she said she was going to ring my neck, so when I told her I was just dabbling the ring leader who was ease dropping asks me was I into the stock markets and I say to him I don't affiliate myself with thugs and crooks then he gives me that dirty look and I just move away. It took me three days to prove my innocence but in the meantime my face was splattered all over town. Now I'm a persona non grata and to make matters worse I lost my job, got kicked out of school, but on the bright side I had a date with Sally, she's one of the escort girls but she's only been in the business two days so that doesn't count. Omg you should see her, voluptuous and hot is all I can say. That's her at the bottom of my page. Moral of the story when you dabble be careful when you need a screw cos you might get screwed at the end. Ciao Jimmy

Aerosmith—Dude (Looks Like A Lady) (# 14 1987)

I sometimes posted my prank stories to my friend's channels and here is a reply from one of them!!!

I just couldn't wait . . . so I had to come here to read the rest of the story . . . you poor thing . . . next time you need a screw be more careful . . . hahaha You are too funny my friend, always bring a smile on my face or make me laugh in tears . . . thank you . . . !

Folks, when that incident occurred my real name was Dick Hurts and my face was plastered in every newspaper in town and featured on every news channel on TV. My family name was mud, in fact my mother was telling everybody I was an adopted son, and my sisters all changed their names cos they too didn't want to be associated with me. And that judge who threw the book at me thought since I was there for two screws I was planning one of them there three way sexcapades; you know a tre ménage something or other. Hey they can all believe what they want, all I know I was there to get two screws. So I had my lawyer change my name in fact they did me a favor who wants to be called Dick Hurts. In school I was the butt of everybody's jokes, they would say "how's tricky Dickie" or "here comes big Dick," or "show me what you got big boy", and the girls called me "hammer on the block." So now I get no flack I still sign my name Dick Hurts but that's cos I am what I am and no Tom, Dick, or Harry is gonna change that. Thanks for hearing me out, btw please continue calling me Jimmy, enjoy this song by The Animals they always equate me with that song, all because I went to the house of ill repute unintentionally.

The Animals—House of The Rising Sun (# 1 1964)

Hey I hate to brag but some folks like to compare me to Mr. Bill 'Bojangles' Robinson cos when I hit the floor something happens to me that's unexplainable. I do a soft shoe routine that has me spinning around in midair and bouncing like a jack rabbit. Do you believe in reincarnation, why I ask is because I believe I was Bill Robinson in a previous life, and if you think Fred Astaire was any good you should have seen me? I could do it all, jitterbug, scat, soft shoe, the lindy, the hucklebuck and the list goes on and on. Heck I was the mambo king not Perez Prado that copycat. Here he invites me to a party and all he had in mind was to take credit for that dance well that's ok cos nobody does it better than me. I was thinking of applying for that 'Dancing With The Stars' but there's nobody who could stay up with me, so you know that's out. Enjoy Shirley Temple and me in this clip, now she had potential ciao Jimmy

Bill 'Bojangles' Robinson & Shirley Temple

Folks recently I met this girl omg she had the prettiest blue eyes this side of heaven. She was walking down the street singing this song, snapping her fingers and I nearly lost my mind cos I couldn't help noticing she was winking at me, either that or she got something in her eye, let's go with winking. So I asked her to come up for a night cap. I know that was bold on my part, but you see my daddy once told me you don't bring knives to a gunfight, what the heck does that got to do with her, well if you should happen to even say a word to her, I will kill you. You know what happens in those night caps, one gets to kissing, then kissing leads to dancing, dancing leads to more kissing and kissing leads to dirty dancing, you ever heard of the horizontal mambo, I nearly invented it. Well gotta go, she's a calling me probably wants to shower me with kisses and whatever else she's got. How does 36, 24, 36 sound to you, yep my daddy would be very proud of me, ciao, Jimmy

Manfred Mann—Do Wah Diddy Diddy (# 1 1964)

Check out this reply below from a dear friend!!!

> I always love your channel Jimmy. You are such a creative spirit; there is not one man like you out there! Wishing you a beautiful day filled with passion and love, Adieu . . .

Folks I'm jumping back on the saddle, no not that, I mean the pole, you see a few weeks ago I had to bow out of Mr. Pole Dancer 2011 competition all on account my package came out, what's that, my nuts and all you freaking morons. Now you know why they say "how's it hanging," well at the time it wasn't meant to be. I had a wardrobe malfunction that ruined my chances of winning the title and getting my name up in lights in Vegas, and you know what happens in Vegas is supposed to stay in Vegas except they blasted my picture, b-s and all, smack dab on the cover of every Vegas newspaper in town. But anybody who knows me knows failure is not an option in my book so I'm back and bigger and better, no besides that, don't remind me. Ciao gotta go practice take care and in the meantime let my friend misshoneyrider1 show you how it's supposed to be done, Jimmy

misshoneyrider1—Dog Days are Over . . . :)

Folks I'm going into the tabloid business as a news reporter where I reveal the dirt and rumors going around and I don't even have to interview anybody just pick a name and presto I make him or her the person of the hour. For example I can say Charlie Sheen is dating a set of twin sisters, yeah he wants to keep it a family affair hahaha. Pick another, John Mayer, good choice, I can say he's replacing Hugh Hefner, cos the old one ain't working like it used too, heck he's dating one gal, what happened to the three he was gallivanting with. And since Mayer is a rock star you know he's gonna party like a rock star. Pee Wee Herman, oh, he's been rumored to play Dirty Harry, don't ask but we can say he's good with his hands. I got plans to be bigger and better then Jerry Springer and Howard Stern and it's gonna be racy and trashy. Enjoy Timex Social Club they know about "Rumors" too, ciao, Jimmy

Folks here's a lovely reply that put me on cloud nine, nobody has ever told me anything sweeter, check it out!!!

> Omg Jimmy, beside your daily jokes I like your latest background. ROTFL :) As I stated earlier, **best of the best, since sliced bread & pockets on T-shirts!** :)

Folks you know that laughter is the best cure for whatever ails you so take my advice and get these two movies, parts one and two, to share with your loved ones this coming Christmas. I do every year and we never tire of it, it's the gift that keeps on giving. And may I be the first to say I wish you a Merry Christmas and a Happy New Year from me and mine to you and yours. And may we all live in peace and harmony and no more hunger or needless deaths throughout the world . . . . Jimmy

Home Alone (Parts 1 & 2)

Folks that's Barry White currently featured on my channel, damn don't he look good, must have gotten one of them there liposuction jobs. I would recognize him

38

anywhere, he reminds me of an actor, no not Jackie Chan the other fellow, see I'm good with faces it's the names I suck in, don't tell me it's at the tip of my tongue it'll come to me later, enjoy Barry ciao, Jimmy

Money Talks (Part 1) (1997)

I got it, I got it, it's Denzel Washington, see I told you it'll come to me, always does

Folks do you recall that story about me joining a nudist colony cos they all thought I was a hunkie, well I fooled them. I'm no more a hunk than those boys from 'The Big Bang Theory,' but I'm here to say dividends are paying off big time. See I was minding my own business laying there naked on the ground when this voluptuous hottie came out of nowhere and sat down next to me and we got to starring and I being suave and macho, but how did she know that, I told her how much I loved her big brown eyes hahaha that's not all I loved. Later tonight I'm gonna drive that woman home and get this I don't have a car or a driver's license and we ain't stepping out of my crib, don't ask. Well I gotta go, getting me a tan all over wanna look my best for when I get in the driver's seat, take her to places she didn't know existed hahahaha enjoy The Cars, ciao Jimmy

The Cars—Drive (# 3 1984)

Hey I'm looking for a woman to be my partner in a new comedy series involving two zany characters, a male and a female who are extreme opposites and each one looking to be in the other ones shoes literally. You know like Sonny & Cher. I be Sonny and you be Cher and I would have it no other way, although I would look better in knee high stilettos but I'll pass for the moment. See we could be the gay guy and the gay girl duo. But in all reality we should have been born the opposite, me a girl and you a boy. Now it gets more complicated cos I do behave feminine and you the macho type. I cook and clean and you are the welder, and ass kicker, and cuss with the best. I sew, you hang in the bars. I watch soap operas, and you go to the fight games. I cry when we watch sad movies, you hoot and holler when that occurs. You wear men's colognes and I ladies perfumes.
Pt. 1

Pt. 2
You wear combat boots and men's boxer shorts, me high heels, panties and silk t-shirts, and stockings. But there's one drawback we are in love hahahaha and we make love like there's no tomorrow; in the kitchen, in the halls . . . and at all hours of the day, we shower and or bathe together, that's a must. And get this; we are so loyal to each other, never a second thought of cheating on the other. Now anyone interested contact my office right here at the love man channel and send me photos of yourself in your birthday suit. Don't worry it's for my eyes only and remember I'm the gay guy so I'm not really into naked sexy voluptuous hot blooded girls, so now that I set the record straight send the pictures over to me. Oh, did I mention frontal and back, good, hope to see ya, all of ya hahahaha bye bye Jimmy

Dave Mason—We Just Disagree (# 12 1977)

Auditions for my partner of crime is still on going, so far 389 applicants, no takers yet so keep them photos coming in. Will have to make a decision soon, must go over them glossy's again for the 13th time it's so hard for me to decide. Heck if it were up to me, I'd let you all take turns with me but keep them pictures coming in cos I need more photos of other hotties, ciao Jimmy

Btw, you can call me Hef . . .

Folks the only time I hate traveling is during holiday seasons cos it's a mad house. If it's not one thing then it's another. Well these two knuckle heads are doing just that and they bump heads time after time. Martin & Candy what a combo, they're just a take of all the other great duos, Laurel & Hardy, Abbott & Costello, Martin & Lewis, Sonny & Cher, and you and me hahahaha. Can you picture us on the road fuhgettaboudit we would be at each other's throats and may the best man or woman win hahahaha. Enjoy the clip in the meantime ciao, Jimmy
Planes, Trains, & Automobiles (Montage) (1987)

theloveman11378 Folks do you know why I have a successful track record as a love man cos I have the ability to wrap my body around a woman's and make her beg for mercy. Why's that, cos I am a contortionist, you know double jointed in eight different locations. Sometimes I do get so tied up that I have to wait a while to a certain body part of mine shrivels up and that can take at least an hour or two or three and that's a pain that hurts so good, don't ask. Well that's why they love me, cos I come from out of nowhere and yes you don't wanna know. See we interlock at certain places and it's an experience and feeling most women never had the pleasure unless they were the ones stuck to me hahahaha. In fact you heard that song by the Spinners "The Rubberband Man," who do you think gave them the inspiration for that song, yep yours truly check it out and every time you hear that song think of me all tied up, Jimmy

Ps
Don't ask, I know what you're thinking, you want a shot at me hahaha

Check out this reply below from a good friend!!!

Hehehe Rubberband Man, love it. Hope you are having a blast darling and enjoying your day so far. No one can make me laugh like you do and since laughter is an anti-aging thing, perhaps I should spend more time with you. Ya a gorgeous, talented, and cuddly soul. Love you bunches, adieu . . .

Yes sweet darling put your ears and lips a little closer to the phone cos what I've got to say is only for your ears and mine, and do send that boy a packing cos this bronco will be driving you home tonight. Let me start off by planting a wet one smack in the middle of your sweet lips, yeah there too. Pretending is not my thing, we'll be mooing the whole night through till the other llamas come home so maybe we should lay down on the hay here in our coral and get comfy and then I claw you up against the railing and do what I do best, need I explain or draw you a picture I hope not . . .

Jimmy
Jim Reeves—He'll Have To Go

Here's a reply from a dear friend!!!

Well my Jimmy boy, sweet honey, my dear hoby, you are right, that song did put tears in my eye, yet the picture capture my laugh I simply cry and laugh in the same time. Have I told you lately that "I LOVE YOU? I just did :):) You are a medicine to all of us, the laugh you put on all your friends is pure health my Jimmy. God bless your heart . . . muahhhhhhhhhhhhhhhhhhh¬hhhhhhhhhhhhhhh just loving you.

Folks you hear that song currently featured on my channel, well this is gonna be my breakout hit and one of my many claim to fame songs cos starting today I'm gonna audition it in all the talents shows, American Idol, X-Factor, Amateur Night At The Apollo. It's gonna make me rich and famous. Girls will be throwing their panties, bras, and phone #'s on the stage and you know what it's gonna get me, panties, bras and phone #'s, you freaking morons. Here check this out:

"BABY LOCK THEM DOORS AND TURN THE LIGHTS DOWN LOW," yep that was me singing them there lines, see I told you I can sing like the best and to quote Tina Turner, I'm simply the best. And when I hit it big I'm gonna buy Graceland and become the new King of Rock 'N Roll. Heck I'll be bigger than Elvis and Daffy Duck put together and let me give a shout out to all my fans.

Love ya all Jimmy, the Country Boy
Josh Turner—Your Man

Another sweet reply from a dear friend!!!

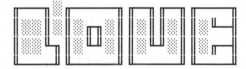

You and your funny stories hehehehehe XXME

Yes folks that's me alrighty, well not me exactly at the moment but the girl I want to look like, see I took that photo to my plastic surgeons and they promised I would look like her. Go down to the bottom of my page to get a better close up view. Omg I'm gonna be one hottie and it may look like I'm a lesbian but I am a lover of women, I'm still a straight man don't let the outer shell fool ya, straight all the way. Ciao Jimmy, the love man, repeat the love MAN, and I may just start loving myself if I look that hot after them doctors get through with me, ooooooooooo weeeeeeeee!!!

41

New version of a previous story slightly changed, enjoy, Jimmy

Folks I've decided I want that sex change after all. Why, good question, cos I got a thing about ladies boots and in order to wear boots around the house, to bed, or to work at the lumber yard, I will want to feel pretty all day long. No, I'm not coming out of the closet I still love women. In fact there's a bonus for me I will be able to go to the ladies locker rooms and take showers and steam and sauna baths and look at them in their birthday suits, hahahaha. I know it sounds crazy but I thought of this all night long. In fact my fortune teller said I was due for a change. See she knew about this before I knew about this what a coincidence, what coincidence, my due for a change, what don't you understand, I'm gonna be a lady wooooo hooooo. Hey do any of you girls out there in You Tube have any extra ladies boots you don't want or want to sell to me real cheap. Hey, size ten in man's size guess that would be an eleven in woman's size.
Pt. 1

Pt. 2
Btw do me a favor keep this to you cos I don't want anybody making any derogatory remarks cos I can be a mean bitch hahaha pardon my French. And get this, I'm going for a boob job, a butt transplant, botox, and you know I'll need electrolysis to get a Brazilian waxing on both my lips hahahaha. Girl, I will be drop dead gorgeous, and don't feel left out go have something done yourself, a nose job, a boob job, heck whatever floats your boat. Do you know that this also calls for, a wardrobe change. Gonna have to buy me some panties and bras; cos a man's gotta do what a woman wants, enjoy Nancy she's got plenty of boots, ciao Janie fka Jimmy the love man, now the love woman

Nancy Sinatra—These Boots Are Made For Walking (1966)

Ps
When the girls and I get together in the sauna rooms we'll be discussing recipes and I'll say I love me some peaches and cherry pies. Hey, do you belong to a gym can I come

Check out these replies from my friends' one's from Ireland somewhere!!

No bootsy they do not, especially naughty men that are lookie-loos lol lol. Behave yourself and sit up nice and straight!

Hello "Jimmy the love man, now the love woman" I got news for you—a man's boots size 10 it is 12 or 13 in ladies (depends on the style), so I wish you luck on finding that . . . you'll probably need a special order . . . hehehe

You don't need a sex change; why don't you buy the boots and just wear them, oh my God this really made me laugh so hard, I can imagine you wearing ladies boots . . . Lol

Hi Jimmy or should I say Bootsy! You make me laugh so much. I'm glad you are here on YT and I love when you stop by and leave messages on my channel, makes me smile and I enjoy reading them.

Your YT buddy . . .

Nooooooooooooooooooooo don't become a woman hehheheh x

Folks for those of you new to my channel I'm a gun for hire. I'll kill anyone you want me too, but you must know I don't come cheap, if you need an ex-lover, an ex-husband, an ex-anything then I'm your man. I can do it in one of two ways, the slow way or the quick way that's your prerogative. Do you want him/her to suffer, well then I'll pull out all their nails, fingers and toes and then chop one limb at a time but if you prefer I can do it quick so they don't know what did them in. Blow them up, drop them from an airplane, believe me it's quick and fatal they'll have a heart attack before they even hit the ground. And get this, for two or more I give a discount. Hey, tell all your friends about me, then maybe you shouldn't it might get into the wrong hands, ciao and you can start calling me Kemosabe, my code name. If I'm not available contact Tonto, omg you should her, that's her at the bottom of my page, ciao Jimmy, aka Killer.

Leonard Cohen—I'm Your Man

Here's a reply from a dear friend and I can read between the lines, I think she loves me!!!

Well if you say so dear, hehehe You could be the devil himself and I would still say he is my man because I know that there is nothing more beautiful than your love, your heart, your mind, your soul, your imagination.

I will always call you my man. Leonard sings it best though honey.

Let me know when you are ready to be swept off your feet. You are like an addiction of the best kind because your love keeps getting better every single day. Loving you!!!

Here's a reply from another friend, I must have told her I could take her to the moon and back, quess she's taking me instead hahahahahaha

Hi Jimmy lol my bags are packed fire up the rocket ship . . . .
... (Y)....
♥(^.^)....
...(")O(")....

Folks I got a story you're not gonna believe a few years ago my girl left me for another. So to get even I decided to knock down her house you see my cousin 'Two Fingers' Lefty owns a demolition business, oh you don't wanna know what he really uses it for. I'll tell you on one condition you don't divulge what I'm about to say or your numbers are up and I hope your insurance premiums are up to date. He works

for the Don, he makes bodies disappear well enough of that. I told Lefty I had a little job I wanted to do so he lent me his demolition truck, its 20 tons and has a huge wrecking ball used to smash down buildings. You guessed it, I'm gonna knock down that low life ex's house down to the ground and she might as well put up a parking lot or a pickle factory cos that's all it'll be good for.
(Pt. 1)

(Pt. 2)
Omg you should have seen her face when she got home, she almost had a heart attack she's lucky I didn't smash it down with her in it. I'm a descent kind of guy why kill her, all I wanted to do was to frighten her. All that remained standing was her front door and the three steps leading up to the door. I left it in case she gets any mail. Last week I saw her on the street collecting cans to make ends meet at the shelter she now calls home. I reached deep into my pockets and gave her a quarter and told her it would help make ends meet hahahaha. Moral of story, don't ever leave me hanging if you know what's good for you, ciao, Jimmy

Amy Grant—Big Yellow Taxi

Folks I got me one of those gismos, I simply plug it into the wall and off I go. See when I come home from work that's when I need that contraption the most. My kids get upset cos it makes so much noise and the bed goes up and down continuously for hours at a time. My grandma who lives down stairs complains cos the ceiling above her shakes and rattles, she's just jealous cos she aint got one. This Christmas I'll give her mine and get me a new deluxe model and I can see her now hooting and hollering. My cat likes likes to get in on the action and jumps on the bed and she can't get enough of it. I think all beds should come equipped with a built in model. I kick it up a notch when my girl comes over for the night she wants one too. I told her she can share it with me, just gotta come over when she wants some. I wonder what it would do for our sex life, fuhgettaboudit, it'll drive you up a wall, ciao Jimmy

Mrs. Brown's Boys—Winnie Wants a Vibrator

Check out this reply to this story above!!!

Oh Jimmy, stop that freaking dirty talk . . . lol.
If all beds would come equipped with a built in model, we wouldn't buy anything else . . . hehehe. Have a lovely Sunday and thank you for the share . . . :)

Folks I got another story I want to tell ya, but hold on to your hats fellas, and you girls, you better tie a knot onto your panties cos this will blow them away. My grandfather was a bit crazy or a drunk or both cos he did the unthinkable he committed suicide. How, good question, he shot himself directly underneath his left breast. When my grandmother got wind of this she was so depressed that she decided she had to join that old fool so the very next day she asked me to fetch her gun. Me, I was too young to realize what she was up to so I did as she asked. Then she told me to 'go now' and as I walked out the door I heard a bang or a bing don't recall exactly but I think it was more like a thump. See she tried to do what my grandfather had done; she shot directly under her left breast. We had to rush her to the hospital, she shot her kneecap. Hey be good or be good at it, ciao Jimmy

The Moody Blues—Go Now!

Folks, today marks the 5th year since my release from the penitentiary, I don't mind telling you this cos I'm a changed man. All those eight years, three months and one day I was locked up all I could think about was people got to be free. I hated being paraded all around that prison yard and frisked day in and day out. I think that's how guys turn fruity, you know they lose their manhood and start jumping rope, weaving baskets, and making pottery. I had dreams of being something big, a pole dancer, a lap dancer, a ballerina guy, anything. Why was I incarcerated, cos I broke into women's houses for their lingerie, heck Victoria's Secrets was my inspiration. I loved the feel of them satin garments all over me body and I would pretend I was a Victoria's Secret model. Hey, mums the word, enjoy The Rascals they too wanted to be free, I didn't even know they were up in the big house until they put out this song, goes to show, you never judge a book by it's cover, ciao Jimmy

The Rascals—People Got To Be Free

Folks I went to my fortune teller just the other day cos I was in the blues and before she could tell me my future she demanded her 50 dollar donation, yeah she calls it a donation so she don't have to report it to the IRS. Then she whipped out that bowling ball that she calls her crystal ball, it's a bowling ball alright just painted up in silver to make it look authentic. Then she puts on her meditation act and proceeded to tell me I was gonna meet a lady of high caliber, smart, witty, charming and stacked to the brim. Oh man when she said that all I could think about was that song "Brick House" by the Commodores. You know that lady with the winning hand 36, 24, 36. Yep a full deck with an awesome set of head lights and a rear suspension second to none. So I asked her how will I recognize her then she gave me the evil eye, she wears a patch on the other and said don't you understand by stacked to the brim. Oh I see, but really I didn't. So I asked her one last question what does she do for a living, she's a writer of romance and spiritual works. Ooooo weeeee sounds like my kind of girl. Now when I'm out in the streets or stores I look at all the women who are stacked a few of them wanted to knock my lights out with my staring. All I hope is she's a writer of X-rated books cos then I can collaborate on my experiences as a hunk and get some, don't ask hahaha

Commodores—Brick House

Folks I got some good news to tell ya, remember that story I told you yesterday about that winning hand gal, yeah the 36, 24, 36 hottie, well let me tell you how I found her. I was minding my own business had to pee so I went around into the alley way and who do you think I stumbled into also peeing in that alley this hot chick and after we exchanged our hellos as we pee'd I introduced myself to her and guess what she's an aspiring writer whatever that is, she writes X-rated porno books. Ooooo weeee I'm in love just what the gypsy ordered hahaha. Gonna meet that crazy chick after work so don't wait up we're in our collaboration period so I won't be back right away we got lots to collaborate. Now what to wear, you know I like to impress, I'm crazy like

45

that, maybe my Halston pink spandex outfit or my Guess jeans with my white go go boots in case she wants to go go. Hey I'll tell you all about it tonight, but if it gets hot and heavy, you know dirty, may not be home for days, maybe weeks, ciao Jimmy

Patsy Cline—Crazy

Love this reply below, hahahahaha!!!

. . . you got to be careful when U go to those alleys and do your thing . . . . hahaha . . . . one of these days u will get a big surprise . . . . hahaha . . . U have no idea how much I laughed with your story, you are a real comedian story teller Jimmy . . . . real funny indeed sweetie . . . . I wish u a gr8 day and don't drink so much water, if u know what I mean? Lol

Hugs n kisses, T.G.I.F.

Folks I got a bunch of e-mails wanting to know what became of my encounter with that hot babe, well I'm here to report chapters 1, 2, 4, & 5 are complete. What about chapter 3, omg you don't wanna know cos then if I tell you then you won't buy the book. That's when we got down and dirty hahaha, no, we didn't mud wrestle but that sounds kinky and fun too. Can you see us now in our thongs and G-strings in the middle of that wooden whatcha ma call it wrestling, shoo we might end up making love all over again. Oooops, I let the cat out of the bag now you know what we did those two days of sin and pleasure. Oh that girl is special, buy the book when it comes out you will learn a thing or two or three. Now the hard part, picking a title, let's see, 'The Hunk And The Hottie In The Back Of The Alley,' or 'She Blew His Brains Out,' oh well that can hold off for some other time gonna meet that gal tonight for chapters six through ten that's when it gets intense, the massage, up on the roof, on the beach, in the elevator, oh when we finish this book it will not only be a best seller but it will win everything, a Pulitzer Prize, Oscars, American Music Awards, ciao enjoy the song . . . Jimmy

Ray, Goodman & Brown—Special Lady

Please check out these two replies below I think one of them has got a thing for me, hahahaha!!!

. . . I have to give it to you. Your comments make me laugh. LOL Thanks for the smile.

Hahahaha you are the funniest man I've ever met. Thank you for sharing your awesome videos with me . . .

Folks I got a story you're not gonna believe, I'm a member of 'The Let It All Hang Out Nudist Colony.' I told you, you weren't gonna believe me. I was butterfly collecting out in the woods when I climbed up a tree to position myself to catch them fly's. Oooo weee what did I see, naked girls and guys, four girls to every one guy. So I sat there for a few hours, four to be exact. There were short ones, tall ones, skinny ones, fat ones, all colors and shapes. When somebody hit a ball my way they spotted me and invited me to join cos they could see I was a hunk. Now every 3rd Saturday of the month I high tail it to the club. I go into the complex incognito just in case there are folks who might recognize me, I don't want anybody calling me a pervert but you know what happens in those places people get horny and I might turn into one hahaha. Hey maybe you wanna join, don't worry I won't tell, we'll hang together, play frisbee, ping pong, fly kites, volley ball, and whatever else turns you on to me, ciao Jimmy

* A re-release of a previous story, a little bit extended, enjoy, Jimmy *

Folks I got a story to tell you, when I was thirteen I fell in love with my home room teacher, Ms. Lee. I would get up early, brush my teeth, take a shower, comb my hair, put on some underwear I found in the hamper and slap on my daddy's Old Spice after shave. No, I didn't have any hair to talk about, heck I didn't have any on my dick either, maybe some fuzz but you'd need a magnifying glass to see that. If you wanna know the truth I was a late bloomer but let's not talk about this here let's just say I was special, yeah that's right, special, I even wore a football helmet to sleep, still do. So off to school I would go and I would pass by the fruit store to swipe an apple for Ms. Lee but what I really wanted was a watermelon but can you see me now trying to stick that watermelon under my shirt and the rest of me skinny as a long neck goose. Any way I would put that apple on her desk and there I am smiling from ear to ear with my hands crossed on top of my desk. Omg I dreamed of her, you don't wanna know hahaha. What became of her, she's a pole dancer in some strip joint, getting lots of tips, don't ask, the cold cash ones you freaking idiots. Hey, check out this song "Mr. Lee" and imagine it being about my woman Ms. Lee.

The Bobbettes—Mr. Lee

Folks can you keep a secret, I found out where Ms. Lee pole dances, I'm always sitting up front and I hoot and holler the loudest and I give her my tip, don't ask, scroll down if you wanna see her photo, thanks and I hope you like the song and Ms. Lee, ciao, Jimmy

The Bobbettes—Mr. Lee

Folks after much planning and scheming I've come up with a game plan on how I'm gonna be rich. I know I told you my luck is gonna change but as a plan 'B' I'm going back into my entrepreneur ways. See there are many folks in need of a soul-mate so I'm starting my own match making business if it can work for me imagine what it can do for you, oh its mind boggling just the thought. See what my fortune teller did for me, scroll down to the bottom of my page, yep that's my soul-mate ooooooooooooo weeeeeeeeee, was I right or was I right, that pretty young thing is mine all mine. Well getting back to my game plan, I figure since I got so many friends in You Tube why not set them up with you folks. Hold up, I know what you're thinking well think no more cos I plan to make you some money too.
Pt. 1

Pt. 2

Every time some new person comes a-knocking on your door you get a cut of the profits. What does 125 dollars sound to you and some days you'll have 3 or 4 or 5 prospects knocking on your door? Hey you don't need to go out with them unless you want a swell time and you'll be wined and dined and a movie to make your heart go giddy up. Maybe a Broadway Show or simply a walk on the beach or just making conversation and if you're not please or find that person nor worth your time then tell them good bye, you get to keep that cold cash and I'll find them another. Soon you'll be singing "I wanna be rich" hahaha, ciao Jimmy, the match maker

Savage Garden—Soulmate Invitation

Another sweet reply!!!

. . . You just made me laugh my head off. : L

Folks let me ask you a question; have you ever won anything in your life, neither have I. In fact the only two times I ever won a thing was when I threw a quarter into a fish bowl and won just that, a gold fish after spending 25 dollars to win a fish worth 50 cents. The booth attendant must have noticed me crying and put that quarter in the bowl cos she felt sorry for me When she told me I had won I nearly fainted and the time I won jack pot in bingo but so did 25 other folks so I had to split that 500 hundred dollars with each getting 20 dollars. See I have bad luck but I know my luck is about to change and when it does you won't see nor hear from me ever again cos I'm getting me a piece of the pie in the sky and will be taking a round trip around the world. I may start with a visit to the French Riviera, they say the ladies there are the most in their birthday suits. Then I fly over to Brazil and get me a beauty queen.
Pt. 1

Pt. 2

And I will be riding high on that float when the Carnival comes around. I will be wearing a thong and a face mask, so you won't know it's me. Then I hop over to the UK, where ever that is, I think it's in the Caribbean somewhere, then Hawaii, the Polynesian Islands, and Vegas is a must, cos what happens in Vegas stays there, you don't wanna know. I'm a hunk; well take my word that's what I am, hunkie dorrie at that. Look at it this way who do kings hang with, no besides hookers, other kings. Who do the rich rub shoulders with, no besides girl escorts other rich people. So I being a hunk I'm gonna hang with hookers and girl escorts. No, you won't catch me with other hunks cos I'm a straight man. I want to be with hotties with the bodies that don't have what I have and I got it thank you. Ok wish me luck and say a prayer for me, ciao Jimmy

Calloway—I Wanna Be Rich

Hey, anybody new to my channel may not be aware that I'm a professional auditioner, no really. See when they were making that 'Dirty Dancing' movie I tried out for the lead, they gave it to some unknown, Patrick something or other Swayze. Oooo I was so mad. Well I'm in the movie just the same that's me getting down and dirty with that hot chick. Well enjoy Crazy Elephant they too can be freaky at times but they're my home boys, ciao Jimmy and do enjoy my 'Dirty Dancing Playlist.'

Crazy Elephant—Gimme Gimme Good Lovin' (1969)

Hey if there's one thing I can do is getting down and dirty, I will have you begging me for mercy hahahahaha. But you'll never know unless you give me a try. I'll take you for a test spin around the block, 60 in 10, and 180 around the bend. You know what they say, never bring knives to a gun fight, well I will blow you out of the water, lord have mercy, good god in the morning, at supper time and, and . . . . Hey must I draw you a picture, use your imagination. Ciao gotta go, but like Arnold, I'll be back!!!

Love this reply from a friend, and she's hot like me!!!

Hey hey! Your comment made me laugh my head off. : L Oh whoa what an amazing comment you gave, was a long one but I love it because I do that too! XD Ah on the BBC you know, haha maybe I will be on there one day. : P Of course I will remember you! : P So how are you anyway? Ah and no problem about the invitation, I came across your channel and could not help but add you. I am Zeba by the way, nice to meet you. Where about in the United States are you at? "Giggle, giggle." . . .

Folks I don't recall if I told you that I did some counterfeiting in my time. Well it's not something you wanna brag about cos I am still wanted in two continents, no not like I'm popular wanted, more like they wanna put me away behind bars wanted. Let me explain, I got my hands on a # of money plates, no I can't reveal my source, yes those metal plates inscribed with the actual faces of real legal tenders. I came up with the scheme of having a double faced legal tender. For anybody who doesn't know what that means, its money you freaking morons. I printed on one side an ounce, well in Scotland sixteen ounces is called a pound and on the other side I printed a yen. Now you know what two continents, Europe and the one Japan is sitting on, I think it's called the Far East or Asia, or maybe down under. Wtf I ain't ever going back to those places. Pt. 1

Pt. 2
My geisha girls and my lassies will have to come visit me here in the Eu Es of Aye. Why a two sided legal tender, good question, this way I can pack my money belt to the extreme and not have to worry of them finding the evidence and to make it easy for me when I travel to those two countries back and forth without being caught as I smuggle them in. I printed a few mils, millions that is. Scotland Yard and the Japanese police are in hot pursuit of me and if they want some of this they will have to kill me cos I have no plans on going to the hokey pokey. What's the hokey pokey, let's just say that vicious place where you should never bend down when your soap slips out of your hands cos those convicts go ape when they see a hole and it won't be mine. The real reason I printed up that money was cos I want lots of it, it can buy me everything and then some. Ask Barrett Strong he too loves it, can't get enough, ciao, Jimmy

Barrett Strong—Money (That's What I Want)

Folks today I wanna tell you a story about blind dating. You see many individuals try to hook up with their soul-mates in numerous ways, the two most common are through internet match sites or in bars. You know those so called clubs where you fill out a questionnaire so the system will try to find you an ideal mate. So if you prefer tall dark and handsome, or black where you never go back, or hung like a brick house, those sorts of questions. Me, I would say, rich, stacked, and witty. Color, if she doesn't have what I got then that's a go for. See when you do use those match sites you really should be honest if you're looking for a sexy companion spit it out, or if horny is your game that too, don't beat around the bush, hahahahaha pardon the pun but I don't have the nerve so I use the old fashion techniques. I hang by the tomato counters at the supermarkets. When I see a girl who I may like I might ask her if she could kindly help me choose the right tomatoes cos my blind grandmother sent me to get some and get some I want hahahaha. Or I do my John Wayne impersonation and try pick up a missy type gal.
Pt. 1

Pt. 2
So as I see one coming my way I say "Ok partner, me and Corky are free and single, how's about we ride you home so these perverts don't hit up on you." How's it going, well I never tried it? Well other ways of meeting the opposite sex or the same sex is at shopping malls, supermarkets, at bingo halls, in the parks, in the beaches, and the most popular of all, in the bars. See that one you have to be careful cos once you start a drinking you let your guard down and you just might pick any Tom, Harry, or Dick cos by this point you're so drunk and horny any thing on two legs will do. Well let me tell you about my blind date, my grandmother set us up, her name was Wanda, the milkman delivery lady. I was to meet her on Saturday night, I get all dressed up, took a shower, shave, put on my granddaddy's Old Spice after shave and some new underwear, well at least clean ones, you never know where this will take you. So I put on my jockeys or fruit of the looms skin tight briefs, that's important cos then you'll impress her with that bulging lump exposed if you should hit a home run.

Pt. 3
So we meet up at a little Italian restaurant two miles away, don't want the local folks to know we're on a date. So I ordered one slice of pizza for two and two glasses of water and then I rapped my heart out. Told her how beautiful her eyes were and that she smelled great, I threw a quarter into the jukebox and put on a soft romantic song, "What's New Pussy Cat" or "It's Now or Never" and I stared into her eyes and when she started to blush I asked her to the dance floor so when she got closer that was my signal. I said we really should be going home and she said the night is young, yes we should, your place or mine. So I took her to my place and I tried 'The English Patient' maneuver and presto we're in for the night. Can't say any more cos what we did was too damn vulgar and sweet hahaha, byeeeee, Jimmy

Btw, she brings me her milk and cookies every day at 4 AM sharp for free haha, don't ask
Tom Jones—What's New Pussy Cat

Folks, there's another thing I want to tell you; I'm a junk collector, like Fred Sanford & Son I go out at night scavenging for junk. You have no idea the money folks put out on the sidewalks and I have my steady route. I go to those rich neighborhoods and score like a bandit, but I must warn you there are setbacks. I found this old piano and I had to hire six guys to load it onto my truck and when we got it to my home one of the guys dropped his end and a 1000 roaches popped out of nowhere. I had those guys stomping and at first they hesitated but when I mentioned a bonus, you should have seen them jump up and down, can you picture us doing the cucaracha mambo. We killed most of them but every now and then a new colony pops up and my house stinks of roach spray. I can taste it in my mouth, ooooo don't ask. So if you're thinking of going into the junk business take it from me, don't bring any garbage 100 feet of your home. "Thata thata thata that ta," yep that's the theme song from Sandford & Son, byeeeeee Jimmy

> Girl, I got something to say to you and only you, come closer, what I want you to hear is personal. For your love there's nothing I wouldn't do cos you're my world, my reason for living. All the diamonds and pearls and all the gold in Fort Knox couldn't buy your love, you're priceless, more valuable than any Mona Lisa or any other work of art. You're what the poets and composers have in mind when they write their master pieces. And as for me, I would climb the tallest mountains; swim the deepest seas just to be by your side. You're all I think about 24/7, every second, every minute, every hour, every day, every week, every month out of the year and you're even in my dreams. I would give up my life for you, give you my heart if you were in need of one then I could be with you forever and a day. So what am I saying, I'm saying 'I Love You,' 8 little letters that spell out 3 words, that has 1 meaning. Remember this number, 831, for as long as you shall live, Jimmy, Yours Truly
>
> The Yardbirds—For Your Love

> Yes girl, I would give you my all, just tell me your sweet desires and your fantasies cos I can make that happen and then some. A spin around the block and you will want me to go in third gear and then we will burst at the seams hahahaha, don't ask me no questions and I'll tell you no lies, hahahaha
>
> The Yardbirds—For Your Love

Hey, this comment is for the guys, so you ladies step aside for a moment. Guys, I don't possess a plaque on the wall, you know a PHD, nor am I any of those things I claim in my resume but I can say this much I know what a woman wants, no besides that. When they come knocking on my door asking me for advice on matters of the heart I'm like the "Handy Man." I've been around the block thirteen times and that's why I'm an expert in love. You got to give her respect, show her that you love her, listen to her every words, make her feel she's the best thing that ever happened to you. Give her lots of attention, shower her with kindness, flowers, kisses, make her laugh, make her cry from the joy you give her and I'm sure you will get your just rewards, her goodies and then some. Now step aside and let me say hello to that gorgeous lady, your better half. Girl I think I've made my point, let's see if he's the man for you, tell me all about it tomorrow, photos and all hahaha. Ciao, Jimmy, the Dr. of Love

Folks can I let you in on a little secret, I love all kinds of sugar, brown, yellow, red, green, pink, black I don't discriminate cos what I seek is beyond the color of the skin it's what's inside that counts hahaha I know what you're thinking ooooo weeee don't say it cos yes it's the inside that gets me up and running. Let me put it to you in another way. When you're in love what happens to you, well to me I see stars, my attention span is up and my body starts trembling with every thrust and pounding of my heart hahaha and you thought I was gonna say my . . . . well that too hahaha, and remember mums the word, ciao, Jimmy, the love man but you can call me Al or big boy, don't ask hahahaha.

theloveman11378 Folks I got some good news and some bad news, first the good news, today is Thanks Giving Day here in the Eu Es of Aye that's where we give and count our blessings but here's the bad news and you better hold on to your hats fellas, and you gals, you better tie a knot onto your panties cos one of my ex-mother-in-laws is in town and no doubt will be dropping by. She'll say it's to visit the kids but we know it's to get what she can out of us she'd eat us out of house and home if we gave her the chance and she's bound to steal a bunch of things. Last time she tried stealing my refrigerator saying hers broke down, sure it would with all that wine she packs in it; and I still haven't found my electric razor bet she's giving herself a Brazilian shave down there, what for she's the ugliest 'mo fo' I have ever known.
Pt. 1

Pt. 2
I don't know any man who would want any of her goodies, they're probably all pruned up but then again there's a bunch of hoboes down by the junk yard that won't mind giving her a whirl of a time. Well I don't have to be hospitable. I'll feed that old bag and show her her hat and the door once she's had her fill but until then it'll be another day of living hell. That lady is the spitting image of Satan. I hope you too don't get a visit from yours cos mine drives me to drink. She is the nosiest person I have ever met. When I'm out of the room she's rummaging through my draws trying to find out all she can. The last time she came over she caused what a commotion they had to call the cops before I did anything drastic, today I'm gonna moon that b . . . . and if she doesn't go home gonna invite my friends over and let them tell dirty jokes and cus all they want, enjoy Ernie he too has a mean old mother-in-law he wishes were gone, capute if you know what I mean, Jimmy

Ernie K. Doe—Mother-In-Law (1961)

Please note: This comment above was made only in jest, but then remember who she gave birth too, my better half. My mother-in-laws and I are/were likethis. They worshipped the ground I walked on cos I treated their daughters like a diamond in the ruff I would polish them up and they stood on top of a pedal stile so the next time you see your mother-in-law embrace her with a big hug and give her a great big kiss, thank you, Jimmy

Here's a funny reply I got!!

Omg your story about your ex-Mother.In.Law was so funny . . . I got a kick out of it . . . . hahaha . . . You always come with the best ones here . . . funny . . . hilarious . . . a good touch for the middles of the week . . . hahha

Folks I prepared my turkey dinner today, this is what it looks like, go down to the bottom of my page ummmm ummmm ummmm chicken licking good, looks hot and scrumptious don't you agree . . . Jimmy

Ps
You can't have any

another funny reply below!!!

I was planning to eat some turkey here . . . but the only thing left are the wings . . . . did u eat the rest? . . . . LOL . . . .

Sweetie I'm more than thankful to god that I found you in this wonderful world of You Tube . . . . You make my days happier and filled with humor . . . . thanks for being my Beautiful and caring FRIEND . . . . thank God for having Jimmy in my life . . . . Thanks my sweet friend
Much love . . . hugs & kisses . . . . turkey flavor . . . oppppssss . . . and dressing toooo . . . . Hahaha

T.G.I.F.

Folks I got a confession to reveal and it's really the start of my mischievous ways, you don't wanna know. When I was eleven my friend Mickey and I were going to the movies, what movie is immaterial at this point because what I am about to say is so funny yet so unbelievable I still don't know what motivated us to do it. As we were preparing to buy a few minor things to take along, candy, soda, ice cream, popcorn, a bag of chips, Twinkies, ho ho's we bumped into our friend Henry. Henry was part Chinese and part Puerto Rican and not so bright, you know lights on but nobody home and he wanted to know what we were up to with all the party goods. So we told him of our movie plans and asked him if he cared to come along. He responded that he was on his way to the barber shop to get a haircut, and besides he didn't have any money other than the haircut money. That's when Mickey chimed in and said that he was in luck cos Jimmy, me, was a professional barber. I saw what Mickey was up to so I played along,
Pt. 1

Pt. 2
Yeah but I'm still in training. So Henry wanting so bad to go with us looked a bit hesitant but I guess going to the movies outweighed the risks so he said ok. So we took Henry to Mickey's house where Mickey got his father's hair clippers and we tied a towel around Henry's neck, sat him in the middle of the room facing a mirror

and that's when we performed our very first professional haircut. Mickey started chopping away, first from the back section of Henry's neck and then around to the side burns. Mickey had cut the side burns too crooked so it was my turn and I evened them up except one was shorter than the other, so Mickey grabbed the clippers from my hands and evened them out but then the side burns were nowhere to be found. As Henry was looking into the mirror he seemed as though he wanted to cry and after 20 seconds of silence Mickey looked at me and we had to hold back the tears of laughter.

Pt. 3
And that's when Henry got up and said I gotta get out of this place, not even a thank you or giving us a tip. Heck we were doing it for nothing, Henry was our best pal up until this fiasco occurred, why a fiasco, cos we fucked him up good, Henry's last words to us, I'm gonna tell my father on you. Well for the next two months I avoided Henry's window and walked to school the long way around, and besides I thought I could use the exercise. To this day I tell my new acquaintances this story and it always has them rolling off of their feet and when there's a get together Mickey and I always tell the story of the movie we missed all on account of Henry.

The Animals—We Gotta Get Out Of This Place

Check out this reply and I think I got me a customer, well if she knows better don't let me touch a single hair on her head cos I'll do to her what I did to Henry and that's a fact Jack

Hi Jimmy, I already know you are funny, sentimental at heart and now you are a barber!? I will cancel my appointment to get my hair done at your salon . . . and of course ain't gonna be any tip either . . . lol. Thanks and take care, ...

Folks, now you can add entrepreneur to my distinguished resume. My last money maker was my 'mooning' business, you know where you hire me to drop my pants and moon somebody, an ex-lover, your boss, your teacher, or even your mama. And before that my 'Private Dick Services,' don't ask. So now I was thinking of putting up a 'Massage and Brazilian Waxing Parlor' for women only. Why's that, cos I've woo'd so many women in my time and I've notice they all have one thing in common, they like to look trimmed and sharp. So I'm the man that can sharpen them/you up. I take that razor and some scotch tape or whatever tape it is and presto it's all gone hahaha. Then you have that Sinead O'Connor bald headed look. And the good part you get a free before and after photo. Don't worry I won't sell them to those girly magazines, what kind of a screwball do you think I am, don't answer that. Enjoy this Mrs. Brown episode that's how I got the idea in the first place, ciao Jimmy
Mrs. Brown Gets A Bikini Wax—BBC Episode

Folks I have to come clean I am a male model, yep I sit in front of art galleries, museums, art classes, women's hen parties in the buff, yes you heard it right girls, in the nude, and may I say I look hot and delicious, even if I say so myself hahaha. And the good part I can be had just show me the money so tell all your friends, sisters, mothers, aunts and I can be theirs too. Btw I don't come cheap or easy but then a hunk like me you get your monies worth. Call me, 24/7 and I charge double for holidays and after midnight ciao baby, hope to show you my stuff hahaha, byeeeeeee, Jimmy.

Male Model Posing Nude for Art Class

Folks I'm going on a safari hunt looking for some wild cat to satisfy my hunger, don't ask. I'm gonna train her to be at my beckoning call, do everything to me I ever dreamed for, and then some. That's her at the bottom of my page, well once I get her tamed that is, may take me all night, hahahahaha ciao and how, you can call me Bwanna Jim

Here's a reply I got from a new friend when I sent her this comment above, hahahaha!

. . . ahhhh loveman, sure sounds fun, but you know no one can truly ever tame a wild cat.

Folks I gotta tell you something in private, I have one of them there duo personality girls, yeah she can be a devil one moment and an angel the next but I love her just the same wouldn't change her if I could. And the best part she's all that and a bag of chips, ho ho, twinkies, and a ding dong all put together. Why is she a devil, cos when we get to making love she is an animal, oh you don't wanna know what that creature does to me. Let me just say I love it and when she mellows out and becomes a sweet angel then it's my turn to go berserk on her, hahahahaha. Oh you wouldn't understand unless you're in love, I bet you're a devil and angel too. Well gotta go here comes my little devil ooooooo weeeeeee she's got nothing on hahahaha enjoy Bobby Vee he's got one of them too. Ciao and please don't wait up, don't know how long this party's gonna last, hahahaha, Jimmy

Bobby Vee—Devil Or Angel

Check out this favorable review I got from a friend below!!

. . . Sweetie as usually my laughing time with you is endless . . . your stories are so unique and funny that my tummy hurts from so much laughing . . . . OMG . . . . thanks for sharing those moments of happiness and laughter . . . . you are the King of Laugh . . . . and you one bag of chips too . . . . hahaha. Have a gr8 night sweetie and pleaseeeeee keep in touch always. Much love . . . affection and good friendship on the way 4U sweetie l

Folks, people always want to know what do I really do, hahahaha, nada freaking thing except woo all the girls here in You Tube. Omg they are so extraordinary and hot. And they are from all over the world, Spain, Ireland, Portugal, Italy, Romania, Germany, France, Austria, Australia, England, Wales, Scotland, Mexico, Brazil, Columbia, Uruguay, the Philippians, Hawaii, Japan, and even from the Eu Es of Aye. Now if we can only communicate. See we use sign language when they don't speaka English. But as we all know love is the universal language and I give them lots of loving. And those twins from Scotland they are the most hahahaha, don't ask you don't wanna know. They woo'd me, yep got me good and drunk and took advantage of me but that's for another story, some other day, some other song. C ya hate to be ya, byeeeeeeeeeeeeeeee

Jimmy, aka the Traveling Man
Ricky Nelson—Travelin' Man (1961)

Folks I too was a telephone man, failed to mention it on my resume cos it was only for a few months but I must admit the best few months of my entire life. Why's that, cos I had the pleasure of meeting so many extraordinary women and I serviced them all with a smile but after our encounters they were the ones smiling from ear to ear and then some. What was it that I did, I gave them my services, some got it in the kitchen, and some got it in the hall, heck on the floor or up against the wall cos I was there to please till they were totally satisfied. No job too small or too big I couldn't handle hahahahaha, don't ask.

Meri Wilson—Telephone Man

Here's a sweet message I got from a girl across the pond

```
:.·
···◯···:˙.⌒.
¨
 ⌒.⌒(▒▒)⌒
(˙▒▒▒▒▒▒ ')▒▒▒' )Hello you naughty boy lol⌣´⌣ˆ⌣'

│││ ││♥ □♥□□□□ oƒ ℓσ√ε ƒor □o□ □♥2♥
││││││★││Live Your Life ToThe Fullest,
♥And Follow Your Dreams!! ♥ ∞
♥Have A Nice Sunday . . . . xx♥
```

Folks can you keep a secret, I got a vice I'm not too proud of, I'm a junkie, yep hard to the core, a junk food junkie that is. I devour bags of chips, ho ho's, twinkies, and ding dongs but that's just for starters, whoppers, big mac's ain't safe with me cos whatever I can't eat right there and then I eat with my eyes. When I'm chewing and btw chewing is my expertise I sometimes don't bother to chew I just swallow. Swallow anything in sight, and you too if I could. My favorite hang outs are at McDonalds, Burger Kings, Papa Johns, Denny's, Popeye's, Roy Rogers, Red Lobster's, and Eat At Joe's. Well pardon me but I got a date at the 'All You Can Eat Sushi Bar,' and don't wait up I've been known to stay there for hours on end on my junk food binges, gotta go I'm so hungry I can eat a horse and you too. Enjoy this Larry Groce song, byeeeee, Jimmy.

Larry Groce—Junk Food Junkie

People ask me what am I really about, let me begin by telling you my name in Chinese, hold on to your hat's fellas and you ladies better tie a knot on to whatever floats your boat, here goes, Wun Hung Lo. Well having said that I have to admit I know how to treat a lady right. A good woman needs attention, pampering, and good loving, you can call it what you want, sex, to be touched, manhandled but it all boils down to feeling wanted and loved. Some call me the handy man and some the masseur cos my advice or methods really work. When I'm finished they are fully contented and smiling from ear to ear. No I can't tell you any more cos each gal is different from the next. My evaluations and hands on do the trick. You know anybody needing my services send them over, I'm available 24/7, ciao Jimmy

Roy Head—Treat Her Right (1965)

Folks that's my new friend, yes we're only friends we're going to the beach so do pardon our attire. Omg you should see her . . . . and her . . . . , I may not be home for a few days so just leave me messages, I'll get back to you eventually hahahaha.
Bye bye, Jimmy

Ps
Ok, ok that's my lover, are you happy, I am. I'm on cloud 9 and later in heaven hahahaha you don't wanna know . . .

Btw did you notice the new photo I posted at the bottom of my page? Later when we get back from the beach we're gonna duplicate that romantic love scene, but we got to put some clothes on to make it look realistic. I'll tell you how we did later. So now you know we do kiss on a first date, heck we'll be more than kissing . . . Ta ta, Jimmy

The English Patient—love scene 2

Folks you probably all know how skillful I am, well I was thinking of becoming a pole dancer, yeah the first male pole dancer but I got one minor problem I got two left feet. Why's that a problem, see when I'm in midair my feet must move in different directions and here they go in unison, can you see me now trying to do a split in midair and both feet go in the same direction I would lose every competition and instead of them throwing money on the stage they throw their shoes or even worse tomatoes. So I'm gonna try hooking up with the best. My friend Trina Noel Davis, of misshoneyrider1, is my best friend, no she didn't tell me that personally but I love her every moves and then there's my other new friend Zoraya Judd. Maybe one of them can take me under their wings, show me the ropes and whatever else they wanna show me hahaha, no no this is on a professional level there will be no messing around, not if I can help it but do wish me luck, Jimmy

Misshoneyrider1—The Nearness Of You.

Folks I got some bad news to reveal, my pole dancing days are over, I thought I could stick it out, no not that you freaking pervert. I went into competition and I came in last of 20 other guys. I know I shouldn't give up, heck where would we be if Christopher Columbus made a 360 degree turn back; we'd still be in England saluting King George the 21st. Well any way as I was doing my spins and somersaults and whatever else them pole dancers do my package came out, yep nuts and all, don't remind me. All I know I wanted to die. Hey I got to look at the bright side I bonded with a whole slew of girl groupies. I guess they liked what they saw, no not that, my performance, then again maybe it was that after all. I guess when you got it, like I got it; I'm a hunk after all and the breeding type, hahahaha. Hey, do me a favor don't tell anybody about my wardrobe malfunction I would be the laughing stock in You Tube, nuts and all, ciao, Jimmy

MissHoneyrider1—I Want To Feel What Lovers Do

Hey I was debating if I should erase pole dancing from my resume I did give it my all, no not that, my heart and soul. Heck nobody is perfect so yes I was a pole dancer, maybe not any good but at least I did my best to show you all what I had, well you get my drift ciao, Jimmy

MissHoneyrider1—I Want To Feel What Lovers Do

Wow I can't believe this celebrity paid me a visit and left me a kind remark

I'm glad to hear that you will keep pole dancing in your heart Jimmy! Hugs :)) Honey~]

Folks I'm gonna share a story with you, one that I've never told anybody; in another life I was a sheik, no really. I had a harem of girls, all kinds, tall ones, short ones, sexy ones, drop dead gorgeous ones, and I even had a Greek Goddess, traded twenty horses for her. Man, just one look and I was putty in her hands, in fact she was the one that sent my camel to bed and she rode me all night long with her tales that would curdle your toes. I really can't go into detail cos if the other 50 gals knew what we did they would rebel and leave me in the dust and all I would have left would be that stupid camel with the two humps, not the kind of humps I want hahaha no pun intended, ciao, the Goddess is calling me woooo hooooo, so long, Jimmy aka Mr. Sheik Lover Man

Maria Muldaur—Midnight At The Oasis

Folks I got a personal question to ask of you, do you have a secret lover, do you wander into the night to a motel to hook up with your secret lover. Well if you do please tell me all about it then I'll tell you about the gals in my life but no names please, see a gentleman never tells. Well maybe just the juicy parts, where we meet, what we do, how long, and who comes first. And if your story is all that I'll write a tell all book. Who knows, I'll make you rich and famous, put you in X-rated movies. We'll make the circuit rounds on all the TV shows, be on the cover of all the tabloid newspapers, you ain't seen nothing yet, the best is yet to come. Enjoy Jimmie Rodgers, byeeeeee, Jimmy

Jimmie Rodgers—Secretly

Folks you hear that song currently featured on my channel, well I got a secret to reveal, Tina's talking about me, oh you don't believe me go on and ask her and she'll tell you. Yep it was the result of our secret love affair. But by all means don't tell a soul or any of the tabloids cos then my life will be a living hell, they will want to follow me around and do a tell all and you know that's not my style. What Tina and I did stays in Vegas hahaha. Omg now I'm giving you my rendezvous locations well that's all you're getting from me, enjoy my song, or rather, our song, yeah Tina's and mine, ciao, Jimmy

Tina Turner—Simply The Best (1990)

58

Folks do you recall that I invested in a new business, yes I mooned folks for money, and I'm here to report it's a money maker alright. All I have to do is drop my pants and my money maker comes out hahaha don't ask so call me when you want me to embarrass someone. It can be your ex-husband, ex-wife, your boss, your lawyer, your teacher, your mayor, your preacher, your mailman, your milkman, heck it don't matter who just show me the money hahahahaha, Jimmy

Ps
I'm now thinking of opening up an escort business. I can escort you anywhere, anytime, your house, and my house, up on the roof, in your kitchen, hey there's no limit and I do charge extra for over time, no besides that, hahahaha!!!
Jerry Maguire (Tom Cruise)—Show Me The Money

Folks I got a question to ask of you, is it proper to tell a lady that you just met, "I'll paint your toe nails and you paint my toe nails, and then we paint up the town," My daughter thinks that's sexual harassment, heck she's just jealous cos my toe nails keep changing every week and make me look gorgeous hahahaha. Last week the girl I met at Victoria's Secret chose hot pink so my toe nails are looking hot, but then maybe it was better when the previous gal had painted them orange well you tell me. Tell me what; it's ok to ask a girl that question. It always works for me and then we end up with a night cap and, and . . . well use your imagination. Ok, ok make love the whole night through and come up for some air in between, oh you don't wanna know, hahahahaha. Hey, have yourselves a wonderful day and if a stranger should come up to you and ask you about painting your toes nails don't be surprised it might be me
Jimmy

Hey just wanted you to see the new me, yeah I got me a new barber and she makes house calls and there's no tipping allowed cos she charges an arm and a leg, you don't wanna know hahahaha. Ain't I cute, well that's what she said, so what do you folks think, am I a hunk or am I a hunk hahahaha . . .
Jimmy aka Jockomo

Folks there are only two things that stir me up, a good bottle of scotch or a feisty woman. And then I'm at my best behavior, cos once I get to drinking I'm on fire but once I get to making love I'm on fire too, so damn if I do and damn if I do hahahaha. So what's it gonna be today well it's 6:29 in the AM so where I go from here depends on her, but she's got to make that first move, you know, ask me, wow that's a switch, ask me to dance and you know I'm gonna accept and as we get closer and closer and we start the whispering in each other's ears oh good god I'm in heaven. Maybe I'll take her hand and lead her to the powder room and we undress and hop into a smoking hot shower and let that hot water run all over our bodies and get us spanking clean, sure it will. Better say no more cos from here on now it's doors closed and mums the word, bye, bye, Jimmy, catch you tonight, I just know it's gonna be a long day hahahaha.

Folks I get a lot of questions thrown at me, besides rocks, wanting to know if I'm for real. Well if I pinch myself it will hurt so that proves I'm human, hope that answers one of your questions. But let me tell you some more, besides being called the love man, ok, ok besides me calling myself the love man I am single and I love to mingle. So if you're a lady, I only date ladies, I will show you the moon, yep take you to heaven and back. Once you've had a piece of me you won't want any other, so get rid of that dead beat lover cos I will satisfy all your needs. You ever made love on a mountain top well neither have I but if that's your desire consider it done. Oh there's a catch, you want some of this you gotta give me some of that, no besides that, money. I know, I know, money is the root of all evil well I know how to handle it, give me lots of it, that's all I want. Hey it was nice chatting enjoy Barrett Strong he's a ladies man too, bye Jimmy

Barrett Strong—Money (That's What I Want)

Folks you remember that story I told you about me going to jail cos my grandmother fell asleep at the wheel in my bank robbery attempt well I just want to tell you I met some of the meanest, ugliest mo-fo's on the face of the earth while there. But it did teach me a valuable lesson. If you ever have to confront one of them mo-fo's do what I did, kick his ass and then whip all his friends too cos then no one is gonna mess with you and you will be the man in the house. But do yourself a favor, don't drop your bar of soap, you don't wanna know hahaha, ciao, Jimmy

Bobby Fuller Four—I Fought The Law

Folks I got a story to tell you, like Bette Davis I am also a spy. I can tell you stories that will curl your toes and have the hair on your neck standing up. I can't reveal the places I've been to but let's just say Scotland Yard, Interpol, the CIA, the FBI and even that Pink Panther all want me. No not like they are after me, they want me to work for them that's how good I am, but please don't tell anybody cos I also got a lot of enemies and they might try to do me harm. Yep even kill me, so mums the word, I am really a secret agent man, I told Johnny Rivers all about me and he wrote a song about my adventures, I'll post it later. Well I gotta go Batman is calling me and he and I are likethis hahaha, bye Jimmy

Ps
You should see Cat Lady, I'll post her photo at the bottom of my page, and hands off I saw her first

Kim Carnes—Bette Davis Eyes

Folks, here's another tale from my life of adventure; I am responsible for this song that's being featured on my channel cos I told it all to Johnny Rivers. Pretty faces are the ones to watch out for cos once they undress they try to own me hahaha. I can kill a man with just one blow. I'm handy with a machete, cut a head off in one swing. Sharp shooter am I, hold a quarter in your hand 1000 feet away and see what happens. I never miss except for that one time I sneezed, poor fella never knew what hit him, don't remind me. I had to hide the evidence, fed him to my alligators. Hey, enjoy my song, rather our song, don't want Johnny to get bent out of shape or I might do something drastic to him hahaha, ciao, Jimmy, Double Oh Seven, the original one. Sean Connery, who the heck is he, oh, that wannabe I taught all my moves too and may I say too well, he bedded all my ladies that double crosser, but that's another tale some other day, some other song . . .

Johnny Rivers—Secret Agent Man

Folks I got something to tell you that I'm not too proud of, in my profile I told you I was a grave digger well that's half the story, I'm also an organ stealer. Yep, I bury them folks in the AM and then I go back in the PM and excavate their body parts. Why you ask, cos I make a fortune, like automobiles, auto parts are more expensive. If you're in need of an arm, an eye, a leg, a liver, a knee that's where I come in, I pop those babies off them dead bodies and they're yours. Can you use a new brain or a new heart cos the old one is not too swift, then I'm the one you need. I accept only cash on delivery, no IOU's. Call me if you need a body part, and referrals are accepted so let's do business. Btw I'm not just a thief I'm also an organ receiver, that's right, I got an arm transplant but that's for another story for another day, another song, maybe I'll tell you tomorrow but they'll be no arm twisting, bye bye Jimmy

Young Frankenstein—Who's brain was it?

Folks I got some good news and some bad news, first the good news, I'm gonna be a private dick again, the bad news, I will be in and out of You Tube cos that's what a dick does he goes in and out to solve cases, oh you don't wanna know. And get this; I'll be guarding a big name celebrity. I'm not at liberty to reveal her name lets' just say I might be partying to the wee hours with her. Well I think I've said enough, hey that's her calling gotta get into my private dick persona, you know be a hard dick, walk tall and proud and diddy bop. What's diddy bop, walk like John Wayne and open a can of whip ass if the need arises. I'm one bad mother, ciao till later gators, when, like I told you your guess is as good as mine, dicks are unpredictable, pardon the pun hahahaha, byeeeeeeeeeee

Jimmy

Folks I got a story to tell ya, you can add wheeler/dealer to my long list of jobs I've had to my resume. What's a wheeler/dealer glad you asked, I wheel and deal. Let's say you want something, well that's where I come in, I can get you that something. You want to meet a celebrity, no problem. Why last night I hooked up this hot babe with Boy George, don't ask. Last week this girl wanted Chuck Berry's autograph so I contacted a friend who knew a friend who knew a friend who personally knew Chuckie but I did one better got Chuckie to give up his cowboy boots and he signed them too. He wrote to my new ding a ling friend, yours truly Chuck Berry. Hey, you want to meet Clint Eastwood's barber and for the right price I can get you Clint's lock of hair, or Tina Turner's old dancing nylon stockings, or . . . .
Enjoy Chuck Berry with his only # one hit song, ciao, Jimmy

Chuck Berry—My Ding-A-Ling

Folks you probably already heard the latest rumor going around town, Ashton Kutcher and Demi Moore are splitting up. Well they're not the only ones, you can add Mickey Mouse and Minnie Mouse to that list and in fairness to Mickey his comment to Minnie was misconstrued, all he said was "Minnie you're fucking Goofey." Hey, I say that all the time, well not to Minnie you knuckleheads to my lady love, she's the funniest chick I have ever known, floats my boat all the time, you don't wanna know hahaha, ciao and how, Jimmy

The Yardbirds—For Your Love

Somebody once asked me what am I really all about, hahaha well first of all I am a struggling writer have written three books and have five other manuscripts on my computer, four of them are comedies with Gene Wilder and Chris Tucker both playing me in the story lines. Other than that I'm just your average guy trying to put smiles on people's faces with my stories, music, and personal points of view. No I'm not really a lover man, but I do know what the ladies want, me hahaha and besides that they want to be loved and touched. They want the woman in them to come out and be noticed and made to feel they are god's gift to man which is what they are. Thanks and don't be a stranger come on over any time and do share with me your thoughts, your music, and any goodies you got hahaha a photo of yourself would be swell, ciao and how, Jimmy

Folks I don't know if it was Captain Kirk, Mr. Spock, or maybe Elvis who said the world's a stage and each must play a part well I'm destined to conquer the world, I wanna go where no man has ever ventured before, go to far away galaxies and meet aliens especially the female types. No, not the ones with two heads, or like the female spider who devours the male after having her way with it. See my fortune teller told me something extraordinary was gonna happen to me and I can't pinpoint what she means but there's a million trillion stars out there and I need to see them all so I must bid you all fair well. Don't worry I'll take my computer along and continue our friendship but there will be times I will be too damn busy to chit chat, ciao and how, Jimmy

Ps
My first excursion will be to the moon and back, enjoy the song below
Everyone's Gone To The Moon—Jonathan King (1965)

Another funny reply from a friend hahahaha, I guess when you got it, like I got it, I got it!

. . . your stories always make me roll on the floor . . . . hahaha . . . I hope you come back from the moon . . . . I don't want to see you like E.T . . . . go home . . . . hahaha . . . .
Omg Jimmy, please come to my channel everyday . . . cos you and your humor make my days brighter and full of sunshine. Sweetie . . . . how great you are as a friend????? Well . . . . super . . . . super . . . . super . . . . super Friend 1.000%%%%%%%%%%%% . . . No doubt about it . . . Love . . . smiles . . . happiness are all my wishes for you sweetie and a magical and fantastic week 4U . . . Much love and fun times . . . l

Folks I got some good news to tell ya, I've decided I wanna be a cowboy, yep I've been hanging out in those cowboy bars here in the city and I can spit like the rest of them. I'm gonna buy me a cowboy hat; I think they call them a Stetson or a beret or some shit and gonna get me some spurs as well. Wtf I need a change in my life, I've gotten too soft in the middle, and I hear them cowgirls are all that, and then some, that they kiss on a first date and . . . . Well that's all I can say right here but know I'll be tall in the saddle; I'm practicing my John Wayne walk and talk. So if you don't hear from me any time soon, know I'll be packing my rags and heading somewhere out west, no not New Jersey, farther out west Texas or Alabama. Heck that's why I'm learning how to do the hokey pokey, them square dances are the real deal. No more Macarena for me. So long partner, see already I sound like a cowboy, giddy up, so long, happy trails, Jimmy

Johnny Cash—I Walk the Line

Folks it's me Jimmy emailing you from Kansas City and yes Wilbert Harrison was right the girls out here are all that and a bag of chips. I met Annie Oakley, Brenda Starr, Ginger Rogers, and Miss Honey Dew, wooo you should see how they walk and talk, good god. May stay here a while so please don't wait up cos they've invited me to an all you can devour barbeque hahaha and there's plenty of meat to go around, oooooo weeeee. Hey here comes one now, gotta go she may be miss right hahahaha, ciao and how, Jimmy

Wilbert Harrison—Kansas City

Folks my cowboy days has come to end, it ended when that mechanical bull threw me off and I was out cold for two hours so I'm taking up space travel. Yep, I wanna go where nobody's gone before explore the universe and if I'm lucky meet aliens, the female types is really what I seek, I heard they're out of this world. Uncle Sam is looking for some good men and women to take a journey to the unknown so I'm going back to the basics and getting my body in tip top shape cos I already have an excellent mind but the body needs a little tweaking and I should be ready in no time. Hey my first mission is to the moon and back, so let Jonathan King entertain you while I prepare for the unknown ciao and how, Jimmy

Jonathan King—Everyone's Gone To The Moon (1965)

Folks I got to make a confession, I'm not all that I pretend to be, I'm just a con man, simple and to the point. But I do have the knack of satisfying all the ladies I come in contact with, I can be anything they want me to be, a preacher man, a handy man, your daddy, your lover man, heck even your Juicy Fruit Man. See I got what it takes, for instance you're down with the blues, well I can rid you of them blues and give you all that you need. You need loving, well that's a no brainer but I can also take you to cloud nine, you don't wanna know. Ok, ok, I can put you in a trance and you will be one happy camper, you will wanna own me once I get through with you hahaha. Enjoy this song and by all means call me, free of charge, but yes a tip is optional, in fact it's a must, no tip is to small, or too big, and yes I will barter if you ain't got any monies, see honey for money will work for me hahahaha, ciao Jimmy, the love man . . . .

Mtume—Juicy Fruit

Folks I don't know if it's just me but when I dream it's as if I have a split personality I dream of things that might have been or could have been or what I want it to be. See when you dream I firmly believe it's your subconscious reenacting your fondest desires. Heck I can just close my eyes and I see what I want, it's as if I have the power to wish upon a star and my wishes come true. Last night I dreamt I was in the arms of this sexy gorgeous babe and she held me all night long. It was pure heaven, she had on some exotic perfume that had an aphrodisiac hold on me driving me mad but I dared not move cos I just wanted that moment to last for eternity. I wonder what that means may have to go visit my fortune teller real soon if not sooner, thanks for listening and allowing me to reveal this side of me, ciao, Jimmy

Bobby Darin—Dream Lover

My fan again, pretty soon I might have to start paying her, she'd make a good agent!!! . . . thx 4 your funny message . . . I always get a kick out it . . . . always you . . . . the one and only Jimmy . . . . I don't have words to thank U for your beautiful friendship and of course you have to put up with me for awhile . . . hahaha . . . we are like peas and carrots my friend . . . . or in Spanish . . . . like nail and flesh . . . . hahaha . . . I think in English sounds better . . . hahaha.
Have a gr8 weekend sweet heart and keep your spirit up all the time pleaseeeeeeeeeee :-))

hugs . . . kisses . . . smiles . . . . jokes . . . and a bag of chips . . . . hahaha . . . . included and free :):) . . . so don't cry OK? . . . . :):)

T.G.I.F . . .

Folks I got a question for you, is it ok for a short man to be in love with a giant of a lady, why I ask cos that's what has happened to me. See being a midget, 3 feet 9 inches tall, I'm in love with an amazon, she's more than a lady, and she's 6 feet 2. When we go out the folks all stare and their mouths wide open as in surprised, you can see them laughing and making jokes. But when you come down to it, once we get to kissing and making love the difference goes away don't need to draw you a picture do I, well use your god given imagination. Here's Tom Jones he too has a lady of his own and he too is proud as a peacock, pardon the pun, hahaha, ciao, Jimmy aka Jockomo

Tom Jones—She's A Lady

Folks I got a story to tell ya remember when I told you I was a grave digger well that was the truth but I neglected to tell you it was an illegal operation. See I worked as a hit man and when I did a hit, yeah, killed somebody, I would bury two or three bodies in the same grave you know a hole in the ground. Heck it wasn't where I put them in a box, I would just pile them together and then I planted flowers on top, roses, irises, and tulips. Any way that's what I do I killed people for a price so if you want me to kill someone, or a group of people I'm your man, If you want a group rate I charge second person half off and the third person for free but you have to cover my expenses, what expenses, cost of tolls, flowers, bullets, knives, gloves, shovels, hotel room, and breakfast. So what do you say want anybody dead, then call me and hush the word, ciao Jimmy aka killer hahahahahaha

Folks can you keep a secret, well I got a big one, are you ready for this, it will shock you, see those girls currently singing on my channel, yeah The Shirelles, I once dated them all, no not at the same time you silly goose, individually. I know I'm good but not that good, heck by the time I get together with the third one I would have been too darn pooped to pop if you get my drift. Now Shirley was fine but not the only candy in the store, Beverly was sweet as molasses. Doris, oh lordie lord you don't wanna know, and Micki, what can I say she was all that and a bag of chips. Hey don't be spreading this out cos if anyone asks me questions I will plead the fifth and don't make me tell them no lies. Well thanks for dropping by, ciao and how, Jimmy

The Shirelles—Baby It's You

Please note: I was the inspiration for this song, hahaha yeah when you got it, I got it

Folks that's Billy Paul singing "Me And Mrs. Jones" well it beats falling for Mrs. Brown, you know that crazy lady or should I say man or whatever on BBC but yes I tend to fall for the wrong kinds of women. What is it that I get hooked by them? Is it because they are much more mature and know what a man wants. Enjoy the song and if you got the right qualifications, single and free, not blind, nor in a wheel chair, then call me or better still send me a letter with your photo in your birthday suit, gotta see the goods hahahaha, bye bye, so long, fair well, Jimmy aka the love magnet.

Billy Paul—Me And Mrs. Jones

Somebody once asked me, "Jimmy why are you so different then all the other guys" hahaha, I said cos I am a rock star second only to Elvis, Julio Iglesias, and then some. I party with the best of them, Tina, Linda, Oko, Mick, Bruce, Rod, Billy and Paul McCartney, heck I got it going on but we gots to be extra careful, oh wrong reply, I'm hot like an oven. When I make love I make love and they come back for some more of what I got. So that's me to a 't' hey don't tell my mama cos she'll smack the living s@58 out of me. She thinks I'm a pastor, but don't want to break her little heart . . .

Ciao, Jimmy, aka pastor fuzz hahaha . . . .

Folks I'm looking for a few good men, ok, and women too, see I'm going into the 'Pet Ransom' business. Last week while I was strolling around the neighborhood I saw a bunch of signs posted on the trees asking if anybody had seen this dog and that's when it hit me. I could hijack a pet for money. You know like a car jack or an airplane hijack. Well it's the same thing except you grab a cat, a dog, or a bird, heck even a monkey if that's what they got and then wait for the reward signs to go up. Now how do you price the ransom? Boy that's an easy one, if there are a lot of signs up then that means the owner wants that pet back desperately.
Pt. 1

Pt. 2
Now if too few signs go up, than that tells me they are not too concerned. Maybe a child in the household is the only one who wants it back. The parents don't care cost it's just another mouth to feed that they can do without and they put up the signs to

make the child feel they are doing their best but we know the real deal. So if you want to apply for the position let me know. In the meantime enjoy "Who Let the Dogs Out" by The Baha Men, c ya, ruff, ruff, Jimmy

Ps
Hey does anybody know where Lassie lives; now that would be a goldmine if you catch my drift, hahahaha

Folks to jump start my 'Kidnap a Pet' business to test the waters, I've posted a picture of my cat Pookie aka Goldie, see her photo on my Avatar, with a reward of $5,000.00. Well that was the worst thing I could have ever done. Now I get folks knocking on my door with any ole cat that has an iota of a resemblance, they even tried dying a cat's hair to make it look like Pookie. Heck people were knocking on my door at all hours of the day and night, man I couldn't sleep a wink. So then to put a stop to this fiasco I posted another sign saying Pookie was found, so please don't come to my house, reward was paid out and besides I won't be home.
(Pt. 1)

(Pt. 2)
Second mistake, now they're trying to burglarize my home. Now I gotta get me a ferrous dog that will deter any more robbery attempts. I guess those thieves thought if I could pay out a handsome reward then I must be fully loaded. Yeah fully loaded alright with a shot gun ready to use it in case you have other ideas, ciao, Jimmy

Baha Men—Who Let The Dogs Out

Yes folks people got to be free. I put a notch on my lipstick case for every day I was in the big house and now I can't pack my nail polish and my lip gloss inside of it cos the case has more holes than a women's prison, don't ask and please don't remind me cos now I can't come over to your house to paint your toe nails and then you mine so we can paint up the town or at least rip the roof off your joint hahaha . . . .
Ta ta, Jimmy

The Rascals—People Got to be Free

When I was a kid I went to camp every summer and that's how I got to see cows, horses, chickens, and roosters. I had another name for them there cow tits, I called them milk duds. Well having watched this scene from the movie 'Witness' I got to learn the correct terminology, they are tits. When I was a bit more mature, thirteen, they let me hold them and squeeze them, yeah both of them, you just can't do one and they sort of felt rubbery and I enjoyed grabbing on to them and I must agree with Harrison Ford they are hugemongous, the biggest tit's I've ever held too, don't ask hahaha. One time somebody dared me to get under that cow and squeeze them tit's so I could drink some of that milk, must tell ya it was sweet as honey and finger licking good too, Hey enjoy the scene I always get a laugh out of it, ciao, Jimmy

Witness—Harrison Ford (time for milking scene)

Folks I got a story to tell you that will knock your socks off, today marks the 13th anniversary of the death of my 5th wife. See we were in a car accident and she died instantly and my arm was badly hurt that they had to amputate it. Yep it was hanging on its last nerve. So as they were harvesting all her organs I asked the doctor if they could do an arm transplant which would benefit me in two ways. I would get a new arm and at the same time she would be a part of me forever and a day.
(Pt. 1)

(Pt. 2)
So after that 45 minute, 25 doctor assisted operation it went off without a hitch. The only set back would be that it would be a little shorter, a whole lot smoother, and hairless compared to my other arm, but who cares as long as I can do what I do. What do I do, I beat the meat in the back of Tyrone's butcher shop, don't ask. A few months later on a follow up visit the doctor wanted to know how was it hanging, no not that, my arm you silly goose. And I said fine except I got one problem, every time I go to pee the hand won't let go. See I knew you weren't gonna believe no how, ciao Jimmy

Love this reply!!!

. . . hey some wax could fix the problem . . . . OMG you and your funny messages is like a good glass of milk before I go to bed . . . . hahahaha . . . . where are the cookies? . . . I want some . . . . Never change sweetie cos U are out of this world . . . . no one will be like you so unique . . . with an endless imagination and storyteller skills . . . . hahaha . . . . have a good night and wonderful dreams . . . . and please . . . . take care of the other arm . . . . hahaha . . . . there is a monkey donor . . . . hahaha with a lot of hair . . . . oppppssss . . .):)

T.G.I.F.

I don't know if I ever told you but I have the uncanny ability to speak in numerous tongues, no really and I also know how to fit in. For example when I'm in a Spanish neighborhood I do what the Romans do when in Rome I speaka Spanish. Here let me prove it. "I got sumting to tel jew, wen I partee I drink only da bes, I drinka Heineken o Dom Perignon." Now when I hang with my Italian friends this is what I say, "ay paisano como sera, fuhgettaboudit I'm gonna make you an offer you can't resist, you can marry my sister and her sister" hahaha.
(Pt. 1)

(Pt. 2)
Now when I go into a black neighborhood I say "hey waz sup my homey" and I give them the almighty brotherly handshake, you know where you extend your hand and do the normal handshake then the side grip and then you raise your clenched fist up in the air. Oh don't get me started we can be here all day. Ok, ok one more for the road, when I meet up with my Irish friends we immediately say "top of the morning to ya" and then we go drink some Jamieson wtf it don't matter if it's day or night just

party till you drop hahaha, c ya, and maybe I'll bump into you later gator!!!! Jimmy, the Greek

I'm gonna tell you something I've never told anybody before, I'm tore up from the floor up. You all heard of Evel Knievel, yep that motorcycle stunt defying crazy man. Well like him I'm like a bucket of bolts. I have so many nuts and bolts in my body I always fail that screening test whenever I fly. Those TAS folks at the airports give me the once over and they really earn their pay, but why did they make me bend over was just too much and it violated my privacy. I got pins in my shoulders, in my knees, and all my wrists, and fingers, not up my butt. I also got a metal plate in my head no not that head, you're thinking that one I got an enlargement so I don't know what that has but it has something and I do hold the record in the Guinness book of records but that's for another story some other day. So yes I am put together and held together by tons of screws, nuts, and bolts. They ought to call me the tin man. Ciao and how Jimmy

> Folks back in the day whenever I was invited to a party mama would drive me there and just one look at the crowd she just knew it was gonna be a hell raiser and would tell me not to go but when I promised I would be extra careful she reluctantly said ok. How she knew maybe cos the girls in their miniskirts and low cut blouses was a warning sign I did not see coming. So I go in and six girls give me a wink, one grabs my butt, and another asks me to dance and before I could respond she pulls me away to another room and wraps her arms around me.
> (Pt. 1)

> (Pt. 2)
> Then she whips out a j and lights it up and pushes it into my mouth and before I knew what hit me my mind goes blank. The next morning when I awaken naked on the floor with three other girls I am starting to feel remorseful cos mama was right. When I got home she whips me to a pulp and that's how I realized she was right from the get go, ciao and enjoy Three Dog Night, their mother's warned them too hahahaha, Jimmy
>> Three Dog Night—Mama Told Me Not To Come

Folks do you remember that Mel Gibson and Helen Hunt movie "What Women Want," well I slipped on a banana peel at the office and when I woke up 8 hours later at the hospital I developed the ability to read women's thoughts just like Mel. I know, I know you don't believe me see already I just proved my point I read your mind, and no I'm not a quack. You want me to prove it again. Ok, let me quiz you, what is your favorite feature on a man, well most woman, 95% of the time want one with a big head, no not that one the other one. Well if you dare send me an email and I'll read your mind but if I'm right you gotta reward me, hahaha, no not with money, well you read my mind, and there's only one correct answer hahaha. Enjoy the movie trailer, ciao Jimmy

You know I was wondering what I can do to benefit mankind with that new power I've inherited. What power, hey did you not see the words that were coming out of my fingertips, that I can read women's minds? If I play my cards right I can write a book on the behavior of women in the gutter and it will revolutionize the joy of sex or the things women want men to do to them. Well you get the point hahaha, no not that point, but maybe on a later chapter I'll discuss the point hahaha, bye here comes one now and I just got to get into her mind and her . . . no comment, ciao Jimmy

Folks did I tell you that entrepreneurship was in my veins from day one. I must have been 8 or 9 when I hit the road and shined shoes. No I'm not embarrassed to say this cos that's how I made money to buy me toys, take my girlfriends out on dates, buy them candy and ice cream and comic books and take them to the movies. I was a big man in town, all the girls wanted me. Well I also met some of the craziest people in the world, hookers, hoboes, politicians and other entrepreneurs. Heck Ray Charles was a shoe shine boy himself and look what became of him;
(Pt. 1)

(Pt. 2)
he's had dozens of hits on the charts and they made a commercial about him having the right one baby, uh huh so he owes me big time. How's that, I hooked him up with a bunch of hookers and introduced him to some big name politicians. Heck maybe I'll even make a Pepsi commercial with him and go to Hollywood and sing my ass off on 'American Idol and maybe they give me a freaking Ford car and I rub shoulders with all those 'dancing with the stars' folks. Hey you never know what I'm good for, something I hope, ciao Jimmy

Four Seasons—Big Man In Town

Hey can I tell you a secret, you know I audition for movie parts but it seems I never get the big ones, so I'm gonna take acting lessons. I know you wanna know how am I gonna pay for them. Well between you and me I have a benefactor. Ok, ok if you need to know the truth I met a lady and she's so into me, that I convinced her to pay for my lessons if she wants some of this, me. You see sometimes it takes some sacrificing to get a head. No not that head, well yeah in a way. So I'm rehearsing all those good scenes, you know like "I COULD HAVE BEEN A CONTENDER, A SOMEBODY", yep that was me doing Marlon Brando, from 'On The Waterfront' and "I'M IN THE DARK HERE," right again, that was me doing Al Pacino from 'Scent Of A Woman.' Oh you ain't seen the best of me yet, wait till I show you my 'American Gigolo' scene it will blow you out of the water, ciao Jimmy

Marlon Brando—On the Waterfront

Folks my acting classes are paying off big dividends I was hired to be the rooster at the all you can eat chicken restaurant, I know it's not much but I get 10 dollars an hour off the books and all the leftover chicken I can eat, and I love me some chicken the closer to the bone the sweeter the meat, don't ask. And she's finger licking good too, hahahaha . . . Jimmy

Folks whenever I want to get the latest news and gossip in town I run over to my barber shop cos those guys know everything and anything. Heck they even know how to balance the U.S. National budget, Obama should come over if he knows what's good for him. Joseppie and

Rolando and Cisco could easily become the next top rated anchormen in America well at least in my neighborhood. Hey, do you wanna know who's fooling around and begetting who and where and when. So yes they know everybody's business. They even told me that my upstairs neighbor Yolanda Benderupper strips at that new bar Whiskey A-Go-Go for tips well that's none of my business but I do have an urge for a cold one might drop on over later, no not what your thinking, just to wet my whistle, c ya, be good or be good at it, ciao Jimmy

Folks can you recall your younger days, no even further than that, your elementary school days. Well I can. Let me tell you about one of my sisters who I consider both a moron and a scholar. Why a moron because when she was in the first grade whenever the teacher would call out her name, Luisa, she would never respond cos she knew herself to be Nilsa, not Luisa. And when nobody in the class would respond all the kids would be turning heads looking for that Luisa girl including Luisa. They must of thought that's one dumb kid. But let me tell you how smart she really was.
(Pt. 1)

(Pt. 2)
See she was very shy to raise her hand to ask the teacher if she could go to the bathroom. No siree Bob so she would just pee right there in that seat and when she was through and felt sticky and wet and or embarrassed she would just move to the chair right behind her. Now tell me she wasn't smart. Brighter than a light bulb that's her alrighty. Well now you know why she was both a dumbbell and an Einstein. See ya some other time with more of my family history secrets, ciao Jimmy

Folks is it just me or do you have somebody who loves to gossip. I mean it can be your neighbor, your husband, your sister, or even your mother. Well let me tell you what happened to me a few years back. I was going to have a hernia operation so I had an idea which sister was spreading gossip to the family so I decided to get even. So I told her I was also having extras being done. I figured since I'm on the table the doctor could spin me around and give me a butt job. You know like a boob job except he sticks them bags in my butt cheeks, left and right.
(Pt. 1)

(Pt. 2)
Then after that he can spin me around again and give me a penis enlargement. Well in reality all I had was a hernia operation. A few days later I called my other sisters and sure enough they knew the whole 9 yards, that's when I busted out laughing and told them the truth. I just wanted to make a fool of that gossiper, and it proved she was the one spreading all my business all over town. Well now you know how I came up with the idea of my sex change operation and all those other enlargements I keep talking about. Thanks for hearing me out and have a good day, ciao, Jimmy

Folks I don't recall if I ever told you I met Ray Charles, yep and we got to drinking, he loved wine, especially Thunderbird, oooo weee. Well back to my story, I was involved in an auto accident, so they rushed me to the hospital a block away, and there he was as clear as day, lying in a bed next to me in the emergency room, my idol. His chauffeur hit a tree and Ray's left leg was badly damaged. The doctor told him they would have to amputate it. Oh I was so devastated I cried. But then I heard the doctor say, but you got the right one baby uh huh, boy was that a relief, ciao gotta go, I'm back on the Sherry, don't ask, Jimmy

Hey now that we're on the subject of mothers, with Mother's Day coming up, when I was a kid growing up in mid-school the kids would not only rank on you, but your mama as well and the funny part they didn't even know your mama, that was the way to hurt you. If anybody has seen 'Remember The Titans' with Denzel Washington the scene in the locker room is a prime example of that, hahahaha. Thanks and god bless all our mothers, it shouldn't be just one day of the year try every day of the year . . . .

I got to tell you a story just like them there mama jokes when guys get together they love to tear people apart. You see there's always a ring leader or two, then you need an audience, so on this one particular day during lunch break they were picking on this new employee whose English was very limited. So after a 15 minute barrage of constant verbal abuse the ring leader says what do you got to say, mind ya this was his one and only opportunity to say something in his defense. So he looks at him straight in the eyes and says "dickhead" and we all busted out laughing, he made his point clear with just one word or is it two, no one, hahaha have a nice day, Jimmy

Folks that song currently featured on my channel meant a lot to me when I was in elementary school. You see I had a crush on a little gal. She sat right in front of me in class and I would always fiddle with her hair, long hair of golden locks. And I know the feeling was mutual cos I would always follow her around whenever we went out to play. She would let me play jump rope, hop scotch, and tag, you're it. Well when the weekend would come I would always get sick. So after five weeks of me being sick my parents took me to the doctor and after every kind of tests imaginable the doctor told my parents that fever like symptom was the result of love. Yes I would be so sad and lonely without my Juliet, oh yes that was her name Juliet. The doctor said the only cure was that I go pay that girl a visit every Saturday and Sunday and he was right I was cured in no time. Bye bye, Jimmy

♥ Peggy Lee—Fever

Folks you remember my friend Mickey, yeah the one who between the two of us gave Henry that haircut of a lifetime. Well Mickey was known as a ring leader, the lowest and meanest of them all. He'd get an audience and they would poke fun at anyone. Let him tell you this story. Hey don't believe everything Jimmy says he's just jealous cos I always get the girls. Well enough of him there was a guy that worked with us at the trucking outfit; we were the warehouse workers prepping all the trucks for the next day's deliveries going out. So Chavos, that's what we called him, his real name was Perez, so I would say Chavos why the heck are you working here
(Pt. 1)

(Pt. 2)

you are too good for us, you're an educated man of the world. And besides, you'll only get your hands dirty, you should be a lawyer, a doctor, anything but a warehouse worker. And the boys are all laughing and Perez knew we were making him the butt of our jokes. Sometimes I would belittle him too much that he would later ask me, did I kill your brother, and then I would just smile and embrace him and apologize for my stupid behavior. Like always he would forgive me and hoping this would be the last of me ridiculing him, nope the next day it would start all ove again. Thanks and Jimmy is lucky I don't reveal some of the things I've done to him, fuhgettaboudit, hey those are my words not his, glad to have met you all, bye bye Mickey!!!

Folks I'm gonna tell you what got me through in corporate America and in life. When you are looking for a job, and I don't care what it is, a proctologist, a plumber, a chief bottle washer whatever, when you go to that interview all I ask is that you come fully prepared. Put on your best suit, and by all means shit, shower, and shave, and be there on time, combing your hair, shinning your shoes, and ironing your clothes is a must but last but not least have a pencil in your pocket. See the latter was what did it for me, I was surrounded by folks with PHD's and degrees up to the yang yang but what they all lacked was a writing utensil and of all the three dozen applicants there looking to get that janitor job I was the only qualified prospect all on account I had a pocketful of pencils. Now I sit in an office at the corner of the building and I got me a private secretary. See it also pays to know someone on the top. My granddaddy founded the place, it's called Hurtz Rent a Car, and my name is Dick Hurtz. You might be familiar with an incident when I was locked up for dabbling, yep when I went to get me a screw, well that's a long story but I did have to change my name to Jimmy, ciao and how . . .

Recently I got an e-mail from an admirer, a girl no doubt, wanting to know what I looked like. I guess she's got interest in the kid, that's me. Well if we still had the 'Old YT' she could easily see I was a hunk, I am short, light skinned, rolly polly. I sport a Mohawk and I diddy bop when I walk or hang with the wild boys, I'm part gypsy and part beast. So you see I'm a hunk alright, correct that, I'm a hunkie dorie. Hey if I tickle your fancy or fit your bill you know where to find me. Ciao and how, Jimmy the love beast hahahaha

Hey I'm thinking of writing my own autobiography. Why, well why not. I'm a star and people like to know how stars got that way, you know rich and famous and world renown. I mean being married 13 times and having rubbed shoulders with . . . , well I better not say but I've rubbed many a shoulders how else could I have made it this far. I've seen royalty, presidents, and Don's, all the big sport celebrities, and broke bread with dignitaries, which ones, all of them. And when I receive a Pulitzer Prize for this book then you won't doubt my words. I can tell you this much I was born at night, no not last night, and it was a sunny day, I can remember it like it was yesterday. Gotta go Oprah's on the phone, what the heck does she want now. Ciao, Jimmy or maybe you should start calling me Sir James, hahahaha

Ok, ok one encore before I depart, when I was in mid-school whenever we had a substitute teacher man that was what we called a holiday. Why, cos we could let our guards down and have fun with that idiot of a teacher. So when he or she turned their

back to us we were hurling spit balls at each other. And if we got caught we would say our name of somebody who wasn't there or if all were present we would make up a name. Mine was Jock Strap but my friends call me Butchie is how I responded. I think that's why not too many subs become teachers any more. The hell they go through is not worth their sanity.
(Pt. 1)

(Pt. 2) And get this; it was a tradition that all the students had to sign a sheet that was being passed around to keep track of who was there. And then he or she would call out the names before the bell rang to signal the end of the period. Well when the names were read out loud we died laughing, names like Dick Hurts, Ali Baba, Lee Harvey Oswald, Annie Oakley, and so forth. Talk about bad, well things haven't changed I hop on the bus and the kids are just as mean with one exception they curse like a jailbird, the n word and d and p word are mentioned nonstop I just wanna choke a few and that's just for fun, ciao and how Jimmy

One last thing before this book goes into mass production and makes me a zillion dollars. I've been called many things, bro, homey, poppie chulo, daddy, big daddy, my guy, killer, scoundrel, thief, jailbird, organ stealer, heart breaker etc. etc. but the best one of them all is 'my friend.' If my stories were about you or I sent them to you know I considered you my friend and hope we never lose this bond. I have over 1800 plus contacts but I can truly say less than 150 of you have made my day over and over and I hope that our friendship will last forever and a day. And you can throw in a tomorrow, and a yesterday, ciao and god bless each and every one of you, it was a ball knowing you, Jimmy

jimmyscomedyshop

LAUGH TILL IT HURTS

SUBSCRIBE

Yes folks that's me Jimmy and Goldie, aka Pookie, I know, I know ain't she hot. Well we can be had, no job too small or too big we can't handle, fuhgettaboudit!!!

C ya next time, your place or mine, hahahahaha, it's gonna cost ya!!!

Folks, I got a secret to tell you, in my profile I neglected to say I'm also a con man, to paraphrase Tina Turner, "simply the best, better than all the rest." Let me school ya, anyone interested in owning a piece of the Brooklyn Bridge or of the London Bridge. Well I'm the man who can make that happen. I know what you're thinking no way Jose. Heck I can get anything you want. You want a moon rock, water from the moon, then consider it done. When do you want it? I'll have it in two days, so enjoy the song, ciao Jimmy

Tina Turner—The Best

Hey Folks I got a story to tell ya, I have to be honest if you read my profile you know I was one mad dude, no really I was, so mad I spent a few years in that state asylum near the funny farm. Well I must tell you I am the best basket weaver ever and I can twiddle my thumbs upside down, in my sleep and that's not the best part, I can catch my thumb in the process so I am also one of the slickest ever, enjoy Napoleon XIV, ciao it's time for my electric shock treatment, yippee!!!!, Jimmy

Napoleon XIV—They're Coming To Take Me Away, Ha-Haaa (1966)

Yes folks that's another of my specialties, I have the gift for gab, I'm a highly successful rapper, I can woo the ladies out of their . . . . well let's not discuss this here; this is a family show in YT land. I get them to come up to my house and get them where I have them, under my control, cos I know what I want and what I'm after. Keep your daughters and wives under lock and key cos there's so many like me out there. Enjoy The Jaggerz with their top # two hit in 1970. Ciao, Jimmy

The Jaggerz—The Rapper

Folks they say that laughter is the best medicine, well I got news for you that's the truth so if you're looking for a good time, no I'm not an escort, come on over to my comedy channel and bring your tissue box cos you're gonna cry laughing. I got every comedy sitcom, the best standup comedians and the ones I don't have I'll get very soon. And by all means take all you want, there's no charge but a thank you is optional, hahaha. See you around and if you got any jokes you want to share send them over. Ciao Jimmy

Folks, that Mrs. Brown once again featured on my comedy channel, it's one of BBC's great sitcom comedies starring the talented Irish comedian Brendan O'Carroll. In this episode she/he has had a few too many and is eating shoop and discussing the robbery of the forking DVD. It's one of my favorite episodes. Come on over and check it out and while you're there check out all her/his other episodes, but let me warn you from the outset, you will be laughing so hard you just might pee in your pants, or bloomers no doubt, ciao, Jimmy

Mrs. Brown Gets Drunk—Mrs. Brown invites Dermot's future mother-in-law for dinner.

Hey folks, that's Mrs. Brown getting ready for a Brazilian waxing, a home do it yourself job. Guess when you got a hot date you gotta look your best, my, my ain't she sweet. This is a popular UK sitcom that one of my friends from across the pond introduced me to. Please check it out you'll die laughing, ciao Jimmy. hahahahahaha

Mrs. Brown enlists Winnie's help after she decides she wants a bikini wax

> Folks that's the late great Bernie Mac performing a standup comedy skit as part of 'The Kings Of Comedy.' He's got his hands full with his sisters kids, the 6, 4, and 2 year olds, and get this, the two year old is the ring leader and according to Bernie she's from hell. Hope you like it and check out Steve Harvey as well, ciao, Jimmy
>
> Bernie Mac—Milk n Cookies

> Hey folks, I got a story to tell you, you just ain't gonna believe, back in the day I auditioned to a bunch of groups as a bass man. The Coasters, The Drifters, The er Beatles, and each time I got turned down, it seems I was too good for all of them cats. Well it was their loss but I rather not talk about it, let's just fuhgettaboudit, ciao and enjoy Johnny Cymbal, he's learning to be one himself, Jimmy
>
> Johnny Cymbal—Mr. Bass Man

> Hey folks, here's a comedy movie that you got to see, starring Bill Murray as 'Bob,' and Richard Dreyfuss, as his shrink, you'll go bananas, pardon the pun. Be sure to rent it or better still go out and purchase it. I promise you, you won't regret it, Jimmy
>
> Richard Dreyfuss & Bill Murray—What About Bob (1991).

> Hey folks, here is a montage of some of the greatest movies ever produced, 100 movie lines in all; I hope you'll find a bunch that you like. Me, I saw almost all of them and they are surely a collector's treasure. So when you're not in You Tube, go see a few of these that I hope will make your day. One of my favorites "I'm in the dark here" didn't make the cut but the movie did, oohwahh. See you around, Jimmy
>
> 100 Best Movie Lines in 200 Seconds

Hey folks, here's another montage, this time of the 100 funniest movies of all time. Hope some of your favorites were included, but then again that's one person's opinion, yours might be totally different, so why not make one yourself. Enjoy, Jimmy

Top 100 Funny Movies of All-Time

Yes folks, that's where I used to hang, with the posse that you see on the computer screen. Ummm, ummm, ummm they didn't say much; but boy could they straddle a woody. Me, I can't surf but I love watching, nothing wrong with having fun with the open sunny skies above your head. Now days I just close my eyes and I can see them all having fun. Big ones, short ones, tall ones, and the waves are just as good. So whenever you happen to be going to the beach please think of me and my little posse here, all having fun!!

California Sun—The Rivieras

Folks I hate to brag but back in the day I was known as The Hustler, why you ask, I could single-handedly dance up a storm with not 1, not 2, or 3, but 4 girls and you are looking at them. Heck, I taught them everything they know and then some but I rather not go there, I was a little drunk and didn't know what I was doing but they say I was doing it good and fellas you would be proud of my exploits. So sit back and watch my girls work, you don't see me, but I'm in the front, all dressed up like Travolta!!

Pans People—The Hustle

Hey folks, this is a scene from the 1968 original movie version of 'The Producers' starring Zero Mostel, a young Gene Wilder, and Dick Shawn as Lorenzo St. DuBois, aka LSD. You got to see the movie in its entirety and if you are lucky enough to find it, you will laugh uncontrollably and then some, I kid you not. There are at least another eight great scenes that will have you hysterically laughing. Thank you for your time, Jimmy!!

Love Power—The Producers—.(Dick Shawn as LSD) (1968)

Hey folks this is the greatest comedy movie ever made, released in 1963 starring the best comedians of the TV screen era. Including but not limited to: Spencer Tracy, Milton Berle, Sid Caesar, Jonathan Winters, Mickey Rooney, Buddy Hackett, Jimmy Durante, Terry-Thomas, Phil Silvers, Dick Shawn, Edie Adams, Ethel Merman, Dorothy Provine and many others as cameo appearances. It's a must see. So go out and rent it or buy it. Thank you, Jimmy

It's A Mad Mad Mad Mad World (1963)

Hey folks, thought I'd put on a show for you, enough of me and my girl. This video currently featured on my channel is Laurel & Hardy dancing to The Archies # one hit song of 1969 called "Sugar, Sugar". It's so funny you will die laughing. Enjoy and if you want to, get up and dance, or sing-a-long that's ok. Thanks, Jimmy

The Archies—Sugar Sugar—(Movie—Way Out West)

Folks, featured on my channel is a scene from the blockbuster movie 'Young Frankenstein' starring Gene Wilder, Teri Garr, Cloris Leachman, Marty Feldman, Peter Boyle, and Madeline Kahn in the 1974 comedy directed and written by Mel Brooks. Hope you enjoy it and see it in its entirety, thanks Jimmy

Young Frankenstein—Sedagive

Folks this is Steve Martin and John Candy at their finest currently featured on my comedy channel. It is one of the many funny scenes from their blockbuster hit movie 'Planes, Trains, & Automobiles.' the ending will have you crying so please do rent or buy the movie it will be a collectors item, one that you will treasure for the rest of your life, ciao, Jimmy

Planes Trains, & Automobiles (highway scene 2)

Check out these two replies below!!!

. . . Re: scene from Trains, Planes, & Automobiles

Hahahahahaha rofl!! Very funny, thanks for the share Jimmy, have a great day, peace and love to you :) **** I am definitely going to get that movie :) I laughed so hard, have a great day, love . . . :)

. . . Re: scene from the movie 'Planes, Trains, & Automobiles'

Well I`ve seen this film too many times that I can`t count, same as 'Home Alone.' I can`t tell you how many times I`ve watched it and still laughed till I`ve pee`d myself, hahaha.

Two of my favourite actors of all times, Steve Martin and John Candy . . . they did make a fantastic double act. John Candy was sadly missed when he died . . . he was so talented.

I loved him in the 'Great Outdoors' and 'Uncle Buck.'

Folks I got to come clean, but you ladies better put a knot on your panties first. I'm not that sweet lovable, charismatic guy you all think I am. In fact I'm the total opposite, I'm meaner than a junkyard dog, you give me a dirty look and I hope your heirs got insurance for you, cause you're dead meat, you'll wish you weren't born by the time I chew you up and spit you out alive, comprende. Hey enjoy the video and don't ever cross paths with me or else you're history and another notch on my lipstick case, er belt buckle, Jimmy

Jim Croce—Don't Mess With Jim

Folks currently featured on my channel are scenes from 'Home Alone (Parts 1 & 2)' released in1990 and 1992 respectively. All the characters were awesome especially Kevin, Macaulay Culkin, who steals the show throughout the movie but Joe Pesci and Daniel Stern were equally great. Enjoy, and go see the movies in its entirety, thanks, Jimmy

Home Alone (Parts 1 & 2)—Top 10 Best Kevin Traps!

80

Hey folks, especially you girls, if I were you before hopping into an elevator or a lift, or whatever you call it, you know one of those mechanical devices that takes you up and down from floor to floor, I suggest you put a knot on your panties, you wouldn't want this happening to you. Check out the video. See ya, hate to be ya, Jimmy

5 Ladies In A Lift In Free Fall . . . !

Hey folks currently featured on my channel is DJ Boonie with the song "Baby Boy." It is not only funny and cute, but romantic believe it or not. Check it out, my friend Emily of EmmRandom was kind enough to post it and share it with us on You Tube. Please post a comment for her and even better still invite her to be your friend, Thanks, Jimmy

DJ Boonie—Baby Boy

Hey Folks that's Robin Williams currently featured on my comedy channel, he is so funny and in my opinion second only to me, come on over and check him out for yourself, and while you're here check out all his other stand up monologs, let me warn you now, you might end up crying from laughing so hard, ciao Jimmy

Robin Williams—Live At The Met (Alcohol/Marijuana)

Folks, I get a lot of questions thrown at me about my brown eyed girl, who is she and how did we meet. Well let me say she's all that and a bag of chips. She's pretty, intelligent, witty, giving, thoughtful, she inspires me, and yes has them big brown eyes that I can't resist. And when we make love oh you can fuhgettaboudit, its bliss heaven. We met one day as she was strolling down the street and she looked so fine and I started making sweet talk and before you knew it I convinced her to walk to my door and then, and then . . . . , well that's as far as I go cos a gentleman never tells; but we've been together ever since and wedding bells are gonna chime one fine day, enjoy Manfred Mann, ciao Jimmy

Manfred Mann—Do Wah Diddy Diddy

Folks I have a story you're not gonna believe but I'm the one, like Johnny Rivers I have the ability to do a whole lot of things. Tell your future; make you do things that will cause your heart to skip a beat. Yep, I can predict the weather, raise the dead out of the ground, make the ladies go wild through my sweet talk and give me all their monies and do freaky things to me, but that's another story, another day hahaha. Hey, enjoy the song, no I'm not the 7th son, 7th of nothing is all I am . . .

Johnny Rivers—Seventh Son (1965)

Check out these three replies below!!!

. . . Re: Seventh Son You been on the sherry again Jimmy . . . . hahaha sometimes I do wonder about you and your bulletins. You shoulda been a performer, definitely you've missed your vocation. ThisYT just isn't a big enough arena for you and your talents, I see it as a stepping stone before you go onto greater things . . .

Ladies giving you their money and doing freaky things to you . . . . hahahaha . . . .
You wish haha . . .

. . . Re: Seventh Son Hi Jimmy thanks for the share great song, have a great day,
peace and love to you :) ***** Hahahahaha the ladies do freaky things to you :)
hahahaha :)

. . . Re: Seventh Son Hey Jimmy, thanks for sharing this song . . . .
And you know what, I believe everything you say Mr. 7 . . . .

hugs

* Folks, here's my resume, gun for hire, no job too small or too big that I won't do, guaranteed
or your money back: *

Occupation: Author, grave digger, prize fighter, military man, private dick, firefighter,
repo man, arsonist, bank robber, embezzler, hit man, singer, drummer, trapeze artist,
tight rope walker, triathlon athlete, con man, ruthless killer, ventriloquist, tango,
mambo, and merengue instructor, secret agent man, midget wrestler, a rapper, a
bass man, gym trainer, and whatever else you want me to be (and who knows what
tomorrow may bring)

* A re-release of a previous story to entertain my new friends, thanks Jimmy *

Folks I got a story you just ain't gonna believe, and you ladies better put a knot on
your bloomers cos this may shock you, I see dead people, and they aren't just dead,
I see them in their birthday suits, that's right, buck naked. I can see everything,
hahaha. I knew you weren't gonna believe me. Old people, young people, famous
celebrities, even notorious killers. So I asked my fortune teller what does this all
mean, am I blessed or am I cursed. She looked at me with her one good eye, yeah she
wears a patch, and that gypsy girl wanted to know if I can see Elvis. See you can't
tell her anything that horny toad has a one track mind. Wow, that gave me an idea, so
I meditated and I asked to see Marilyn Monroe, Jayne Mansfield, Gypsy Lolita, omg
I'm in heaven. Hey get your mind off the gutter and check out Johnny Nash, I don't
know what he wants to see but he see's something, hahaha, ciao, Jimmy
Johnny Nash—I Can See Clearly Now

Check out these replies below!!!

. . . . Re: I Can See Clearly Now dead people

Guess what?? I can see dead people too, for real, and ufo's sometimes, here and there, and nobody believes me either. But I can't do it 'on command' like you, you're quite the psychic aren't you?

. . . . Re: I Can See Clearly Now dead people Hi Jimmy, wow you see dead people and they are naked!!! Hahahahaha that's interesting, well you won't get bored now you have company! What does Marilyn look like? Just kidding :) hahahahaha!

Re: I Can See Clearly Now dead people

Hahahahaha, hey Mel she looks no different than all the ladies out there, I mean she's got what they got if you know what I mean. And you should see my gypsy's mother, never mind that's too gruesome hahahaha. Thanks for your visit, Hey we need to get together and talk politics, religion, and me hahahaha,
Byeeeee, Jimmy

Hey . . . , we should get together and do something, what's on your mind tiga. I can do cartwheels, I can swim backwards and get this, I was once a lion tamer so maybe you should come into the cage with me, don't worry I carry a big stick, if any of them should bite you I'll beat them silly and if I have to use my pistola, that's Spanish for gun. I'm a marksman, hahahaha Well what do you say partner, can I call you that, partner and it's all the red meat you can eat and tons of money. Hey let me know ASAP I got things to do and places to visit, ciao, Jimmy

. . . Re: I Can See Clearly Now dead people

Sorry Jimmy, I'm a vegetarian but that money offer sounds very promising . . .

. . . Re: I Can See Clearly Now dead people

Ha, you're tripping me out! Love it.

Folks have you ever been in love with a Dr. Jekyll & Mr. Hyde personality of a sweetheart. Well let me tell you what happened to me just the other day. We were on a line waiting to see a movie when these three roughnecks tried to get in front of us. Well my gal grabs one of them and not just any one, the meanest, nastiest one of them all by the collar and yanks him to the ground that before you knew it we were surrounded and they beat the living crap out of me. I ended up at the hospital with two broken ribs, a black eye, and three broken knuckles. What's the moral of the story never date a woman who looks like an angel but is really a devil in disguise? Oh we're no longer together and I heard she's doing time for beating up two old men who gave her a wink. Let The Clovers tell you about their experience, hahaha, ciao, Jimmy

The Clovers—Devil Or Angel

See these replies below!!!

. . . Re: Devil Or Angel Well she was not a very smart warrior was she?

One must choose their battles wisely and never endanger others . . . actually saving/helping/protecting others/self, is the ONLY thing worth fighting for . . .
Thanks Jimmy. I love your communication style . . . :)

. . . Re: Devil Or Angel Hi Jimmy sorry to hear you got beat up :(Nasty! Well I can say you are better off without her, thanks for the share of the video, nice song and I had never heard of it! Have a great day, peace and love to you :) love . . .

Re: Devil Or Angel hahahaha, ... hey this was just a prank story only to put a smile on your faces and to introduce my featured song, See I'm in the process of writing a YT book and it will contain all my pranks stories, just look at my comment in my comedy channel you can't believe I'm all that and a bag of chips hahaha, I know it's April fool's day but I've been making silly comments like this for over two years, hahaha, wait till you see that book, hope to complete it in 3-6 months hahaha, byeeeee Jimmy

. . . . Re: Devil Or Angel Hahahaha. Better not introduce me to this sweetheart of yours. She sounds a scary gal. You sure pick em. What movie was it by the way? Dr. Jekyll and Mr. Hyde hahahaha.

I hope those bad men didn`t get you in the family jewels. Especially since you had that arm transplant and that hand won`t let go of your . . . !!!

Put a little steak on that black eye. Kiss your broken little knuckle wuckles, and soothe away your pain . . . hahaha . . . .

Folks add to my resume 'miner' cos I'm packing it all in and gonna seek them golden nuggets; there's gotta be some left over from the year of '92. Me and my woman, Pookie Girl, going way up North, yep "North To Alaska" and if I fail to find any well I got Pookie to give some of her golden treasures. What treasures is that, hahaha her sweet loving and her awesome . . . . . , hey, must I draw u a picture use your imagination all I can say she's got a body worth all the gold in Southern California. Wish me luck or wish me happiness with my brown eyed girl, bye bye and so long Jimmy

Johnny Horton—North To Alaska

Two more replies!!!

. . . Re: way up north, North To Alaska Hi Jimmy hahahaha lol so funny, I did use my imagination :)

. . . Re: North To Alaska Haha, aww Jimmy, you're so cute . . . . good thing Pookie girl is going with you to keep you warm!! They still have internet up there, don't they??

I'll be waiting for that picture you're gonna draw . . . ;)) hugs

Hey folks it's Mother's Day in the UK today so to pay my respects I found the perfect song; but let me first tell you a story. You know I've been around the block thirteen times, three times just to one lady, my shrink. Well in all honesty I hated all my mother-in-laws. Yes they would pry into my business like how much does he make, is he good in the sack, and always giving me the eye like if they could get into my pants. Well it's true they all looked like Satan's mother and always eavesdropping even when we were making love, they had to put their ears to the door and all kinds of stuff. So if you're a mother please, please be a good mother cos if you don't I can be one mean mo-fo and if you keep that up, I will throw you out the door head first, ciao and do enjoy Ernie K Doe, Jimmy

Ernie K. Doe—Mother-In-Law (1961)

Please note: Just trying to pull your leg once again, I fabricated this story to get a laugh, my mother-in-laws were/are sweet loveable ladies and we were/are best of friends, thanks Jimmy

. . . . Re: Mother-In-Law Now that was a bulletin and a half, hahaha I was expecting something nice for us mums, but your stories are something else. I never know what you're going to come out with next. Sometimes it's scary hahahahahahaha

. . . Re: Mother-In-Law Hahahahahaa rofl thanks for the share, funny song! Gee nasty mother-in laws!! The song was truly fitting, have a great day, peace and love to you :)

Jimmy do you have any more funny movie clips to share? I would love them as I love collecting funny videos; I have on order 'Planes, Trains, & Automobiles'!! Hahahahahaha :) have a great day, peace and love to you :) *****

Folks I want to tell you a story that you just ain't gonna believe, I was once arrested and put into a mental institution. How I got there, well this creep tried to hit up on my girl so I took a handful of his throat and threw him to the ground. Oh that's just the beginning, one day I see he's at this fancy Italian restaurant with this pretty girl so to get even some more I come up to the window where they were eating and I dropped my pants and mooned them real good. A cop car just happened to be passing by when they apprehended me and I was sent to the cuckoo's nest. For those of you who don't know what that is, it's the mental institution. I was held there for one month for observation. It was the best month I ever had, that's how I met Jack, yes Jack Nicholson. Well watch this clip maybe you'll might spot me, I did a cameo but no more clues, hahahaha, ciao Jimmy

One Flew Over The Cuckoo's Nest (1975)

Check out these replies below!!

. . . Re: Re: One Flew Over The Cuckoo's Nest [trailer] (1975)

hey they strap you down and then insert a rubber piece in your mouth so you don't bite your tongue or swallow it, I'm not sure and then they take a live wire to your temples and zippey do dah zippey yay, and you sleep it off for the next 24-48 hours,

HAHAHAHA been there and done that, yeh I was sent to an asylum the last time I mooned somebody and it wasn't just somebody, the King of Scotland or of Ireland I forget, all I know it was painfull, no not the mooning the electric shocks, hahaha hey get with the program Missy

. . . Hey the King of Scotland, you mean King MacSporran . . . wow you were lucky to get away with electric shocks, normally he boils those mooners, skins em and stuffs their skins with haggis. I believe it's quite a delicacy he'd have loved a Yankee skin cos they`re a lot tougher than what's he`s used too . . . bit more grizzle in them and all . . .

. . . Re: Re: One Flew Over The Cuckoo's Nest How long ago were these treatments Jimmy, last Friday? Ahhhh that explains it . . . your brain hasn`t settled back into your skull. It's still zippidy doo zippey yaying around.

I know where I`d a put the live wire. And you won`t need three guesses. and loved to have heard you singing falsetto . . . well it would be more screaming than falsetto, cos your notes would be so high pitched they`d be off the Richter scale . . .

, , , Why you're the most lovable Cuckoo of them all, that's which one you are, my favorite nut, Jimmy!!

Hey folks I heard they are looking for actors to play the Three Stooges in a movie revival, so I am gonna audition for lead role. Why me, ok so I don't have the acting qualifications but to be a stooge you have to have the goods, and I got the goods. I'm crazier than a spinning top; I can moon anybody, anytime, and anywhere. The ladies love me and the hoods are all afraid of me. And it you asked me to walk into a lion's nest well you know I'm fearless but I'm not that crazy. So cross your fingers for me, ciao, Jimmy.

The Curly Shuffle—The Three Stooges, Mo Larry, and Curly

. . . Re: The Curly Shuffle Oh woweeeeeeee Jimmy Boy well that's so! Bloody absolutely! Awesome! What more can I say Speechless I am. Good luck and all that stuff that spreads like jelly on bread. Don't keep me in suspenders do hurry tell me they signed you up, err . . . why you may well ask, well err . . . . I want to be famous for knowing someone famous and that be you Jimmy Boy. I knew it, I knew you'd go far mum drilled me with there's always a light at the end of every tunnel. Keep me updated with all this goodness my good friend Jimmy Boy.

Have a safe and great weekend doing your curly shuffle with surprises, sunshine and endless smiles, from your number one fan . . . .
˙··•♥ . . . ♥•··˙

. . . . Re: Re: The Curly Shuffle

aaaaaaaaaaaaahahahahaha crazy? That pretty much sums me up . . . sometimes! But oh boy Jimmy Boy I'm dangerous if you ever care to ruffle my feathers, I'm crazier than the Mad Hatter!

Thanks for the giggles & stuff
°°¤ø,,,ø¤°°`°°¤ø, ĵúŜmėee, being me! x

Yes folks that's Ralph Kramden and his side kick Ed Norton of 'The Honey Mooners' dancing up a storm to The Jive Five's "I'm A Happy Man" on my comedy channel." Well if those knuckleheads ever came to your party they would sure make you a happy man cos you would laugh up a storm watching them make a fool of themselves on the dance floor. The song would reach the # 35 spot on the Billboard Charts in 1965 and in my opinion should have been a top twenty hit. Enjoy and hope to see you around, ciao, Jimmy

Folks, I got another story to tell you, remember that butt cheek implant I had a few months back, yeah it's like a boob job where they insert a sack into each breast well they inserted them to my butt and I'm here to tell you it's paying off dividends. Last week Pookie and I ran off to Brazil and guess what, I took my bathing suit off on the beach and I was the hit of the town. All the chicks couldn't take their eyes off me and I could see they were licking their chops hahaha. Hey enjoy "My Boy Lollipop," yep I felt they all wanted me as their lollipop. Hey ask Pookie she's my lollipop girl. Enjoy the song, a top two hit in 1964 on the Billboard Charts by Millie Small, ciao, Jimmy

. . . . I can't stop laughing at that story, Jimmy, glad that worked out so well for you and your lollipop Pookie girl . . . . hahahaha . . . .

. . . Re: My Boy Lollipop Hey . . . . I did write on my list, that a nice ass on a guy would be a bonus but I meant the real deal hahaha. I don't wanna squeeze no implants . . . Hahahahaha

Folks here's one fecking crazy Scottish man, Robin Williams, featured on my comedy channel, now I know where he gets his comedy ideas, goes to Scotland and hangs with the brothers even those who wear them men skirts, kilts I think is what they call them. I once wore one and the next day I was lying in the front of my house out cold drunk and when I woke up I was surrounded by all kinds of animals all my neighbors were there too. Bet I know what they were checking out, haha, what I had between me legs and guess what, someone tied a red ribbon around my you know what. Guess I must have won first prize for something hahaha. Ciao, enjoy the skit by Mr. Mork himself, Robin Williams, Jimmy

Scotland—Robin Williams discussing the greatness of Scotland

Hey folks that's me and my woman, she's all that and a bag of chips, may have to marry her one day. And if you think you've seen it all, nope, you should see her . . . . and her . . . . Good god, you talk about . . . . . She's got the prettiest set and she's out of this world. Hey need I say more, well I'm not saying, she's mine all mine and you can't have none, ciao, Jimmy

Ps
You want a glossy copy of this photo send me your e-mail address, there's no charge but a tip is optional, hope to see you at the beach, that's right, the nudist one, hahahaha

Folks, that's Steve Martin himself on my comedy channel, well it was me who showed him all the moves to how to dance the Merengue. Yep it was me alright, thank you, didn't you read my profile I'm also a dance instructor, hope you like this clip and do see the movie in its entirety, "My Blue Heaven," costarring Rick Moranis, you'll die laughing, ciao, Jimmy

. . . Wow, Steve Martin's got it going on, I had no idea! You're a great teacher, Jimmy, I'm impressed . . . .

jimmyscomedyshop Hey I too have a Mary Lou of my own and when we went down by that swimming hole, spiders and snakes were not what I had in mind, we got in that water hole buck naked hahaha. Don't need to tell you what happened next, but let's just say I married that girl. Now when we wanna have some fun we just mosey on down to that water hole and yes we jump in buck naked feet first hahaha. Enjoy the song; it would be Stafford's biggest hit of his career back in 1974, climbing to the top three spot on the Billboard Charts. Hope you enjoy, ciao Jimmy

Jim Stafford—Spider & Snakes

Check out this reply from a new friend below.

Hi Jimmy . . . . ahhh . . . I don't like spiders and snakes either. :-))))) I hope you are doing well . . . keeping posting those great old hits. They are the best . . . !! Take care, . . .

Hey folks I got a story to tell you, I have the ability to twist my body in every which way unimaginable, I think I'm known as a contortionist. Well that song currently featured on my Comedy Channel by the Spinners is me to a 'T' cos I am a rubberband man. Yep and it has it good points, I can twist my body around my girl Pookie, yes my brown eyed girl, and she just loves it, hahaha let's just say when we get to loving there's nothing I can't do, say no more hahaha, ciao, Jimmy

Spinners—The Rubberband Man

. . . . Re: The Rubberband Man Hahahahaha rofl Jimmy, Pookie gets the body twists hahahahahaha! Cool video, have a great day, peace and love to you :) ***** I have always loved that song :)

Re: The Rubberband Man Hey that's not all Pookie gets hahahaha, and sometimes we can't untie ourselves I have to wait till my you know what shrivels up a bit hahaha. Yes we're like two dogs in heat stuck to each other, para bing, para bang hahaha. Omg you don't wanna know hahaha, byeee, and thanks for your reply, Jimmy

. , , Re: The Rubberband Man Hahahaha Jimmy you always make me laugh and that is good, hahahaha now I tried not to imagine something shriveling up :) hahahahaha that's funny! :) OMG rofl! :) Thanks for the nice message made my day :) . . . .

Re: The Rubberband Man . . . you too make my day, it's nice funny replies that say my prank stories were not made in vain. I have two other friends from your neck of the woods and they both think I'm a nutter, they couldn't give me an explanation what a nutter is, tell me that's a good word, hahaha

. . . . Re: The Rubberband Man Hi Jimmy, thanks for the video hahahahaha rofl, you have 2 friends other than me in Oz, they think you're a nutter, that's not a good word :(Keep on smiling :) Have a great day, peace and love to you :) Love ya, . . . :)

. . . Re: The Rubberband Man Try not to hurt yourself Mr. Jim

Re: The Rubberband Man hahahahahaha, . . . you're so funny, heck I don't hurt myself I'm in bliss heaven with my Pookie girl although sometimes we can't untie ourselves until you know what has had enough, gotta wait til it shrivels up a bit hahaha, thanks for your reply, Jimmy

. . . . Re: The Rubberband Man Hey Jimmy!! So good to hear from you!!! That's a fun song, and Wow! Your pookie girly is lucky, really lucky . . . . ;))))

Re: The Rubberband Man hahahaha, yes she is lucky, I wrap my body around her and sometimes we can't get unlocked, I'm totally inside of her and we have to wait till we're finished making love and my you know what goes down otherwise it's para bing para bang, hahahaha, Thanks for your reply, byeeeeeee, Jimmy

Re: Whipping Lions Hey Sweet Pea, I'm just a big prankster was just trying to get your attention. Hey do you sing, I could use a lead singer for a new band I'm putting up, after you finish singing I go around and pass the hat, 50 50, 65 for me and 30 for you. Hahahaha, ok so I can't sing but we can still be partners, you're hot, I'm hot, we'll burn the place. Maybe I can paint your toe nails and then you paint my toe nails and then we paint up the town, hahaha. C you around partner, Jimmy

Ps
Check out my other two channels, you'll love them. Hey I also love spiders and snakes, hahahaha, no I mean the song, hahaha Spiders & Snakes, by Jim Stafford

. . . If I could sing I would be making my own music. As it stands, the cats and I have an agreement. I don't sing and they let me live here.

You have some fun channels. Thanks for being a friend.

SP

. . . Thanks so much for the invite! I also subbed. And I really appreciate your "favoring" my Sweet Pea. I am so glad that you rescued a cat. I too have a rescue!!!

Yes folks, when me and the boys finally get our one big hit we're gonna demand that we get our picture on "The Cover Of Rolling Stone" magazine and we'll be so famous, have our own groupie of chicks, and so rich. Rich, heck I'll settle for rich never mind the cover, just show me the money hahahaha. Enjoy Dr. Hook And The Medicine Show with their blockbuster hit song that would reach the # six spot on the Billboard Charts in 1973 ciao, Jimmy

Dr. Hook And The Medicine Show—The Cover Of 'Rolling Stone'

Folks as a tribute to Easter tomorrow I'm featuring this song as a reminder that we are living in a world that is slowly decaying and it's not too late to change it for the better but it has to start at the core of it all. We need our teachers, doctors, builders, and business men to open up their eyes and give from their hearts cos they are the ones who can make a change. I pray that as human beings here on earth we can pave the way so our children and their children will inherit a good earth . . .
Ciao, Jimmy

Harold Melvin And The Blue Notes—Wake Up Everybody

. . . Re: Leona Lewis—Footprints In The Sand
Hello dear Jimmy! It's really nice to have a friend like you on here :))
. . . Thank you for your always sweet and lovely messages and comments! I have so much in my mind, but in English I cannot express that easy what I feel. That's why I try always with my videos to express what I have inside my heart. Because "when words fall, music speaks" And there is no better way to show our feelings than with music.

I love this video from Leona. It's really heart touching, and it makes my cry every time I watch it.
So my dear, please keep in touch!
Take always good care of yourself.
With Love, . . .

Re: Leona Lewis—Footprints In The Sand
Hey Little Angel you sure know how to touch someone's heart, Very nice video and thanks for sharing and for caring, I left a comment, bye bye sweetie, Jimmy

Hi, . . . I wanted to leave a comment on your channel but you don't have it set up that way so here is what I would have said . . .

Girl you are a barrel of laughs, your pole dancer is just one example of your fine works, a little short but funny as hell. I hope you'll accept my friendship and make a ton more we need lots of people like us, Jimmy

. . . Re: Pole Dancer
Poor woman! That's what you get for making an effort . . . while not being as handy as you should. :D

. . . Re: Bobby Fuller Four—I Fought The Law (And The Law Won)
Oh my god Jimmy, this story is sooooooo GREAT :-))). I love it!!!!!! Thanks a lot!!!

You are really the greatest, Jimmy!!!!
And thanks a lot for this song, too!!!
Take care . . . .

. . . Re: Re: Re: Hiya Jimmy Thank you, I'm always happy to listen to good advice, so I appreciate your kindness with the "filling in". Will have you know I am also a fussy one as to whom I pick as friends, that you must now feel honoured :-) Also maybe my astrology birth sign might have a tad something to do with it, I'm a Virgo through' & through' & furthermore, it's my birthday tomoz yeah 2nd whoopypeee \o/ so, sing up & along with me "Happy Birthday to you, Happy Birthday to you, happy Birthday erhmmmmm me, Happy Birthday to me"

Catcha soon & thanks again!!
‚*•.‚*•.‚ *•.‚*•.‚ · · · ‚•*‚•*•*‚•*

Folks I got a story that you're not gonna believe, I was incarcerated, put in jail. One that they tie you in a strait jacket for those they think is nuts. Let's start from the beginning. I have a girl that with her big brown eyes is the center of attention that guys try to hit up on. Well this one particular bird dog wouldn't stop so I grabbed him by the throat and spun him around like a rag doll and he learned not to mess with her again. A few weeks later I saw him in a restaurant with a girl sitting by the window. So wanting to get even some more so I come up to the window and I dropped my pants to moon the son of a bitch, and the cops grabbed me and put me in the pokey in the psychiatric ward for 55 hours. I was charged with disturbing the peace and released for time served. So you see I am considered crazy and a persona non grata. Well that's it, enjoy the song, it's dedicated to my little brown eyed girl who I just adore, C ya, Jimmy

Love this reply to that story above, check it out!!!!

> . . . Haha, oh Jimmy . . . why moon the guy, I thought you would teach him a lesson—not reward him!! And I don't see how you could ever become a persona non grata, my dear . . . but I really love your crazy stories!
> Have a great weekend, sweetie.

Heres a reply I got after sending my new friend the male nude model video!!

> . . . sent you a video: "Drawing Model (Funny)"
> Very funny video, haha . . . :-)))

Here are two replies I got from a new friend when I posted some of my pranks on her channel, we always have fun when we get to chatting and discussing the matters of the heart!!!

> . . . Re: "Wanda the Massage Therapist" OMG! Thank you! That was Awesome.

> . . . Re: "Wanda the Massage Therapist" That was great. I might be on your channel all night! No, I don't think I will get bored. Tess

Hey folks, especially anyone who is of Irish or Scottish descent, I got a question for you, those bag pipers that you see on St. Paddy's Day marching in those parades, I'm sure you know what I'm leading up to. Is it true they wear nothing underneath? Why I ask, I was planning on wearing an outfit like that on Halloween and needed to know the proper attire. I was also thinking of bending down and taking a peep but I'm afraid I might get killed by those guys. An Irish friend of mine tells me they don't wear a thing, so maybe I was lucky I didn't take a peep after all, they would have thought I was a pervert and beaten me to a pulp. Maybe I should go as a pirate that sounds a lot better! So what do u think, do they, or don't they, just want to know for the record. Those Irish people always seem to have a different story depending who you ask. Let me know ok, Thanks Jimmy

Check out these three replies to my kilt story!!

> . . . Hahaha . . . you don't have to be Irish or Scottish to answer that, of course they haven't got anything on underneath. : D that's a well-known fact. How about those traditions, eh? :D

> . . . Re: enjoy, true story so help me Hey Jimmy, I don't know man. I don't know nothin' from no bagpipes, and I really don't know nothin' from no kilts! But hey man, I was working down in N Orleans last year and the band was having lunch together at a restaurant and I overhear the trumpet man telling the piano lady that he used to wear a kilt. He said he wore it for a year but stopped wearing it a while ago. I'm glad that he stopped wearing the damn thing before I had to be standing on the bandstand next to him! That kilt was east village like a mug. But hey, I know that being judgmental is the worst drag of them all, so I say if you want to wear the kilt, got for it! But man, don't look up under when those cats come along blowing the

bagpipes! They're usually blowing for some dead cat and he probably got dead from looking up some dude's kilt!

Ha ha ha ha. Take care and keep me posted Julian

. . . Enjoying HAKA v Kilts.
Remember it's pretty cold at Halloween time.
You might need a hot water bottle in your sporran.
Good Luck lol And wishing you a great week :)

Here's a conversation I had with my friend we're always pretending to be half-brothers, long lost at that and by a different daddy. I guess we're two of a kind hahahahaha!!!

. . . Happy Friday to you
Jimmy my lost brother I'm watching you (the women) what can I say I proud of you stop by to wish you a great week-end hope all is well for you take care Elias
B. T. O.—You Ain't Seen Nothing Yet

. . . Re: Did you find another brother?
Jimmy hello to you haven't heard from you lately so just stop by your one of many channels to wish you a great week-end hoping all is well for you the video I'm send you is from a group here in san jose cal. the bass player is the leader of the group and also a co-worker please comment on the group take care my friend and say in touch if you don't I'm going to tell mother. Elias

. . . Re: Did you find another brother?
Ok you twisted my arm and no need to go to mom. You know how to use the power of blackmail!! I could kill you!!!

Jimmy

Ps
Enjoy Kool & The Gang—Hi De Hi Hi De Ho

Here's a new friend reminiscing how she grew up with my father's idol Carlos Gardel!!

. . . Hi!! Hello Jimmy! I am so grateful for your words . . . I was very excited when I read that your father was listening to Carlos Gardel . . . and I remembered my dad who also is in heaven, he loved Gardel and the first song I learned in my life singing was the tango "Volver", he and my grandfather were great musicians and they taught me to love and respect all genres of music, but the tango here in my country we carry in our blood:)))) Lol!!!

Friend thank you very much for sharing the videos you sent me, great dance of Al Pacino! I have the movie! Receive my love and my gratitude for your kindness Jimmy!
Greetings and kisses: D

I posted a comment on a new friend's channel and this was his reply!!!

. . . THAT WAS AWSOME OF YOU TO LEAVE THE KID A COMMENT

Here's a friend wishing me a good weekend, we do that a lot!!!!

. . . Have a great weekend Jimmy . . . enjoying your channel very much
Lots of my favourite funny video clips

~The most wasted of all days is one without laughter~

Yes folks that's me alright, "The Boy From New York City", but they got it wrong. I'm not tall. In fact, short and stumpy and rolly polly is more like it, fine is questionable. I diddy bop from side to side, oh I'm down alright, tore up from the floor up. Penthouses ha, try a trailer house down by the railroad tracks. I'm not cute nor sport a mohair suit, try polyester, 100 % pure. I have holes in my pockets so obviously there's no spending loot, busted plain broke, maybe a few quarters and Lincoln. And the only thing new is this bicycle I found at the dumpster outside of town. Dance, I got two left feet, Romance well maybe back in the day except when I'm with myself because I can't get a friend who'll put up with me. Heck even a blind lady, or one in a wheel chair, or with 13 toes will do. But yes, I do hope that today you'll make me yours. God I could use a friend or too, I'm way over do. Oh yeah, ohh yeah, ah huh, ah huh, oh yeah.

The Ad-Libs—The Boy from New York City (1965)

Conclusion

Well it's been a wonderful experience these past three years, 4 months and 7 days but who's Counting? I'm glad I took my daughter's advice otherwise I would never have had the enjoyment that You Tube gave me. I've met so many wonderful people, and that includes a sweetheart or two. Thank god I saved a lot of my correspondences and was able to use them to put out this book. I must say it was quite a challenge to go through my e-mails and pick the best stories I could find. In conclusion I have to say You Tube is the best web site for socializing and for collecting videos of all the greatest songs, movies etc. ever made. It is also a sight for posting freedom of speech comments and the reason it's become the best sight for news reporting around the world. I'm not a politician or a preacher man but as long as fair and honest reporting is allowed to be made than that's a bonus. Thank you for your support and hope I've made your day, ciao and how, Jimmy

About the Author

Jimmy Correa is the product of a military life. He was born an Army brat and he and his sisters have traveled the world all over. His father, a career soldier was a big disciplinarian man and Jimmy learned right away the importance of honesty and self-righteousness. He bypassed the opportunity to go to College on numerous scholarships and opted to go to work instead. He worked for a big major Wall Street firm for over 32 years and then moved to North Dakota for eight years where he was able to put out his first book. He admits he learned from his mistakes and each and every time he writes a new book his confidence and workmanship improves so he says. Having experienced the stock market crash in 2008 he has learned to be frugal. He lives with his daughter in NYC, who he thinks is a whole lot funnier than him. She gives him the inspiration he needs to write and he's always working on more than one project at a time. Presently he has five other works at hand and another bunch in his head including some commercial pitch ideas that he hopes to sell to the sponsors. He has written a few editorials and sent the political top brass some ideas to improve the current economic status which includes balancing the budget and getting America back into the market place to create desperately needed jobs. He also has an idea for a TV music game show that would compete with American Idol as the best music show around. I'm sure we haven't heard the last of him. Stay tune act two is just around the corner . . .

My Best Friends in You Tube

(1)

When I count the number of friends I've had in all my channels Maggie ranks as my all-time favorite cos she's made me laugh the most. She is one brilliant writer who I've tried to convince to pursue a writing profession. She's quoted me some of the best jokes, poetry, and Irish blessings that I have ever heard. Nobody could compare to her level, she was one awesome lady who I miss dearly and can say I truly admired. True some of her material was not all hers but the way she put them together and the comments she wrote just blew me away. I have no icon to illustrate her channel cos she's no longer in YT but I will always remember her. Here are some memorable quotes of hers. And where ever you are, I hope you are well and life is good. I just loved her theme:

Live, Laugh, and Love, Well what else is there she summed it up in four beautiful words.

> Hey folks, I am proud to say I just reached a milestone in YT, MayMaggie became my 500th friend, and considering that I ignore many invites because they have nothing in common with me this is an important event for me. I choose friends based on their choice of songs, their profiles, and sometimes on their channel's back ground. I'm not into rap or politics, or religion. Not that I'm against any of them but not what I want to share or debate on my channel. Music is the universal language so I never reject anyone based on their nationality. Thank you for your time, Jimmy

(2)

> Sofia in my opinion is by far the best video maker in all YT. She is so talented and her choice of music is exquisite. I have praised her time and time again; there is no one before or after her. She has set the bar that nobody can come close, second to none. The following are my favorite videos she has downloaded. Check them out if you do have access to YT you will agree she is all that, thanks Jimmy.

THE BEATLES—COME TOGETHER
Sofia you rock, and now the entire world will see what I've been saying all along, the greatest video maker in all of YT that pays tribute to the greatest stars that ever lived!!!!!!!!!

CHUCK BERRY—JOHNNY B. GOODE
Folks this is rock 'n roll at its finest, if I were asked to choose one song to describe rock 'n roll this would be that one bar none. Elvis was King, Celine the Queen, The Beatles the Four Crown Prince, but Chuck was not only a nobleman but a jester to boot. My good friend Sofia is responsible for this video and she's got more just like it. Enjoy the song, ciao, Jimmy

SANTANA—BLACK MAGIC WOMAN
Sofia some video makers concentrate on one particular or maybe two or three music genres, like pop, country, rock, instrumentals, folk, R&B but you girl, you do it all and this song rocks. Your slides were well put-together, it's so original, you go girl, 99 stars for your video, 1 star for Carlos!!!!!

```
___♥♥♥♥♥___♥♥♥♥♥
__♥♥♥♥♥♥♥_♥♥♥♥♥♥♥
__♥♥♥♥♥♥♥♥♥♥♥♥♥♥♥
___♥♥♥♥♥♥♥♥♥♥♥♥♥
____♥♥♥♥♥♥♥♥♥♥♥
_____♥♥♥♥♥♥♥
_____♥♥♥
_____♥ Thanks for all the beautiful comments!!!!!!!!!!!
```

OC

(3)

Marisol is by far the most vivacious lady I have ever met in all of You Tube, since day one she has made me feel so good to be alive. She can liven up a party and before you know it the house is a-rocking. Her stories have made me laugh so hard I hate parting from her and her good will can unite people of all races. Hope you too will get to know her and she will be a keeper, Jimmy

Ps
Now she's the girl I would enjoy being stranded on an island cos she will make me forget my problems and have me laughing all day long. Plus I'm certain she can pamper me with her fine cooking and she'll wash my clothes, fetch me coconuts and go fishing for my food and kill a peacock for my Sunday Bruch, hahahaha

When we get together its pure mayhem, we're the 'new Lucy and Ricky Ricardo' of YT. I plan to write another book solely on our chats, you will die laughing when you see this extravaganza, yes that's what it will be, maybe a pilot for a TV sitcom too, hahahaha, you never know . . .

Jimmy

(4)

Of all of my friends in You Tube Robin has always made my day. It was a constant thrill chatting and swapping jokes, little insults, and making sweet talk with her. She is not only witty but has a heart of gold and I'm sure she is the center of attraction at any party she goes to. Send her an invitation and you will agree she is a living doll.

Hola Jimmy ~ Swinging by to wish you a "Blessed and Safe" Memorial Day weekend. Wow . . . can't wait until after the holiday to kick back with all those coolio shares you've been sending my way. Grazie!!! Have a "chiliburger" or two and enjoy. Talk with you later . . . Chili-V =)

"Baby . . . Baby . . ." Hmm, love your featured video . . . care to dance? As much I love to get my groove on . . . I do love to dance slooowww . . . Wishing you a "fantastico" night . . . Thx for all those shares . . . they make my day and night. Ciao, Chiliburger =)

Tsk . . . Tsk . . . my toes have looked better. I guess it's "Sloppy Joes" for din-din . . . Let's see how you do next time with pedicures . . . Maybe we'll buy finger licking' chicken. Oh . . . I like Ding Dongs for dessert. Yumm!!

Hey You ~ Thanks for the comp's . . . Yeah, music has been a big part of my life since way back. I've been to so many concerts; I've lost count of them all. And yeah . . . I have seen Bad Company. Like you, I can't seem to get enough of the music. You and Me . . . we're TIGHT. True friends are hard to come by

Yo Gilli-Jim . . . stranded on an island alone with you might be fun . . . This would be MY fantasy . . . YOU can build me a lil hut with French doors . . . oui oui . . . then YOU can play like Tarzan and crush the coconuts between your . . . . knees and dribble the sweet milk into my waiting mouth . . . YOU can wrestle with the sea urchins and feed me "sushi." Ahhh . . . a nice back rub would be nice after spending all day sunbathing and waiting for you to finish up YOUR chores. And if you're lucky . . . I might "hula" for you . . . cause this Ginger loves to dance! Then you can serenade me to sleep. Awwwwww . . . =)

Note: This comment above was in reply to The Intruders song "Together." Man, is she just too much, love how she puts words together and dazzles me, love her to death!

Hey I heard a rumor; you're quitting your day job to start a singing career. Well you're in luck I was once part of a band and I can do the moonwalk and do cartwheels and also sing back up. And if you need a manager or an agent I can do that too. Oh I can't tell a lie, I can't sing a lick to save my life but I do hum, now that I'm good at. What you say partner, can I call you

101

partner, partner. Heck I'm also good at passing the hat around, I watch it like a hawk, nobody steals from us . . . And its 50 50, 35 for you and 65 for me and you might as well start calling me BOSS. What'a ya say Robin, and don't have me waiting too long for you to decide, I got places to see and places to go or something like that. Take care, Big Jim!!!!

Jimmy. Jimmy it's gonna cost you to join my one girl band. There's the audition. Besides moonwalking and cartwheeling, I'll need to see how well you twirl on a pole and you gotta give the boss a lap dance. I'll also need to hear you hum "Mambo No. 5" while you sway those hips. HaHa . . . you are a funny man. No way baby . . . if I sign you on as partner . . . it'll be 35-65 . . . me with the biggest cut. Ohhh, I'll let you drive the Hummer and if you prove yourself, I'll throw in a rollaway for free when we stay overnight at the "Roach" motel. So give me a "holla" and let me know if you wanna join the band. Peace Out!!! Chili-V =)

(5)

Connie is one of my favorite down loaders, her videos and music choices are so unique, she has introduced me to so many new artists and that's a treat for me cos I can't get enough of new artists and music. I have reviewed many of her videos and she ranks high up in the top. I created a playlist of my favorite videos of hers, around 70 at last count.

(6)

What can I say about Alma, she's a lady through and through, she is one friend I can't get enough of. We can chat forever she always has a kind word of advice and always makes me laugh with her replies. We are like toast and butter, we go together like ham and eggs. Don't get me started I could praise her all day long, she is a keeper and I adore her friendship!!

(7)

Lisa is my southern belle who is so alive and personifies life. She features so many dance tunes and is a pistol with her sharp and witty remarks. She's definitely one of my favorite friends in all of You Tube.

When you going to learn Jimmy, I will always be one step ahead of you . . . . you might throw me strike, maybe two, but on that third strike I will hit it out of the park . . . . running to first base, oh my second base, still going third base, jumping for joy home run!!!!!!! So u see Jimmy never mess with a LADY she has moves no one knows . . . and a LADY is always faithful to her man . . . . LOL

Whoaaaaaaaaaaaaaa Jimmy, I am sure your girl is singing around the room "I am sure my baby is a magician, cause he sure has the magic touch" . . . . She is one lucky girl . . . . you better hang on to this one . . . . dance all night long with her . . . . hugssssss . . . Lisa

Thanks Jimmy for all ur wonderful comments you give me . . . . you are a true friend . . . . and of course I love this channel . . . . you know that . . . . Jimmy have a great weekend . . . take care, Lisa

Now Jimmy forget about Marie and come dance with me . . . . We can show Marie and Billy Joel how to cut a rug . . . . LOL . . . . that is if you think you can keep up with my dance moves . . . . LOL . . . . Or you can stand back and watch Marie's mouth drop to the floor . . . . LOL . . . . what are friends for . . . . I got your back Jimmy . . . . LOL . . . . hugss . . . Lisa

. . . Re: Re: between the moon and you

you're so funny Jimmy . . . . didn't you learn never to marry your shrink . . . . you can't win in that situation . . . . I know . . . wait . . . . I think I am your shrink . . . . omg . . . three times . . . . where was at . . . . out of my mind . . . spent too much time on that couch . . . . LOL

Re: you're so sweet Jimmy,
You walked into my life to stop my tears and everything is easy now, I have you here . . .

Every time you touch me I become a hero
I'll make you safe No matter where you are
And bring you everything you ask for
Nothing is above me I'm shining like a candle in the dark
When you tell me that you love me
Thanks Jimmy you're my hero . . . the bestest of best . . . . Lisa

8)

Eve is one very talented girl, when I first laid eyes on her channel I knew right there and then she had something going on, her videos and choice of music is so exquisite and diversified; and you never know what she's gonna showcase next and when you think she can't get any better she shines like a beacon, good god, what a talent . . . .

(9)

Elia is another friend who inspires me, she is heavily into fashion and the arts. Her videos are all geared to the fashion world and sexy gals in lingerie. She's one channel to keep an eye on cos she's going places; I'm always complimenting her on her exquisite workmanship, Jimmy

(10)

Linda is what I call this fun loving no nonsense gal who picks her friends like if they were rare diamonds cos she wants the genuine article, ones that will chat with her and not BS, Jimmy

AWWWW . . . . LOL . . . . sorry Jimmy I don't want to be in your gang, I mean band. I can't sing for toffee, just as well cos I don't like the gloopy stuff. And besides another thing your 50 50 cut don't ring too sweetly to my ears, your calculator is nazzed. But best of British Luck in finding a sidekick to make you rich & famous. LOL •*¨*•♫♪♥

11)

Trish is fairly new in YT but when you look at her videos you wouldn't think so. Her videos and her choices of songs are amazing; they go together like a glove. She leans toward romance which is an extension of her home lifestyle, he must be a lucky man that's all I got to say, rock on with your bad self girl, Jimmy

(12)

Lena is one so down to earth gal, she loves life and we've shared many videos and she loves my prank stories. She is so young and will grow in time, her numbers are already impressive and her videos awesome, Jimmy

(13)

Mate, Walter, is one dear friend; he kindly made for me as per my request two songs that were in tribute to my parents, both deceased. He touched me and I could never repay his kindness, one that I will never forget as long as I live, Jimmy

The two songs were "Adios Muchos" by Carlos Gardel his idol and also my father's and "Quantanamera" by The Sandpipers for my mom who passed away in February of 2011.

(14)

Mellissa is so sweet and her replies to my prank stories are just as funny, love her, Jimmy

Btw she is the only person that has replied to every single share that I've sent her and I think that is why I love sending those shares cos she has class and is one very remarkable young lady!!!!

(15)

MissE is another good friend of mine who I enjoyed chatting and is a whip with her brilliant replies. She's one very hip young lady and has made a few videos on her spare time, I've tried to motivate her to make more, hopefully will find the time someday, Jimmy

> Oh Jimmy . . . . so lovely to hear you are so well after your big operation *smiles* . . . I am really happy for you. Just imagine all the good times you are going to have with your new girlfriends . . . coffee shopping . . . OMG!! Are you going to share your new recipe with your friends here??? I am so jealous you have new boots. Might have to go shopping myself. Wanna come?? . . . Well you enjoy your new "freedom" and don't forget to drop in and say hello every now and then . . . Luv & {hugs} MissE xxx
>
> missembar hahaha, you are a nutter Jimmy

(16)

Morgana is such a lady and quite the video maker. She has made some very beautiful videos and her choice of music compliments her works of art. It was always a treat chatting with her, always brightened up my day.

> AH AH AH AH LOL LOL LOL
> Very funny ""joker"" veeeeeery funny indeed XD
> I love your sense of humor LOL. Woo Woo Woo XD
> . . . ✰ . . . Have a beautiful day Jimmy . . . *‿*
> Much Love . . . . *huge hug*
> ☙Morgana♫•*¨"*•.•*¨"*•.❤

Hey Morgana, I am so sorry we parted for a while but after deep consideration I thought we have to be friends we have so much in common but the one factor that influenced me is the fact that I too am a MusiCalCoholic so you see we are joined at the hip after all. Take care, Jimmy

> ❤•*¨"*•.,•*¨"*•.,•*¨"*•.,•*¨"*•❀❤❀•*¨ *•.,•*¨"*•.,•*¨"*•.,•*¨"*•❤.
> Thanks for the compliment to my house and yes we can be friends, but not at the hip my friend, cause my hip is already taken *smiles* and hon, I am sorry to disappoint you (again) but, the Celine Dion song did it for ❤Jack❤
> . . . . ✰ . . . Have a beautiful day friend. *‿*
> . . . . *hugzzzzzzzzz* ☙Morgana♫•*¨"*•.,•*¨"*•.❤

(17)

Barbara or Babsie, a rose by any other name is still a Babsie, is one very delightful lady. She is a fun loving individual and it's always fun and mayhem when we get to chatting. I think she wants me but so do I. Her channel's theme is Andy Gibb and his brothers. I like to call her my kissing cousin cos her dad came from America and I always tease her whenever there's a sporting event involving both our countries. She is one very popular lady and you too will like her but don't take my word for it check her out, Jimmy

Hey Babsie let me ask you a question, during the world cup which team were you rooting for, USA or UK. This is very important because I need to know where is your loyalty is. Remember who your daddy was so be honest, I thought so, thanks, yeah we had the better team and thanks for rooting with me. I'll tell the boys here you are one of us. LOL, Jimmy!!!

> Hey Barbara, it's me again, Jimmy, you heard that expression "the third times a charm," well that's what I do best, charm the folks here with my rock and roll music. They're all inside my jukebox filled to the brim with the greatest rock and roll songs from the 50s through the new millennium and of every genre. What say you come on over and check me out and if I don't mesmerize you with my music then we call it good bye, sayonara, avidasen, ciao. I know you won't because I got what you want, music to blow you away and make you want to stay and come back over and over. Want to make a bet that you will not only like my channel you will love it. And the good part, you can take anything I got and then some. C U around gator and please don't be late, expect you by eight!!!!

> . . . I'm here by eight where's the vodka, you're so bad lol!!!!!!
> loving ya jimmy xxxxxxx

(18)

In my opinion Steve is the savviest Elvis channel in all of YT. His videos are so interesting cos he goes inside and tells us facts about Elvis which most folks knew little of and there's nothing he doesn't know about him. I've tried to convince him to write a book, a tell all, and hopefully one day he will.

Check out this reply Steve gave me!!

> This is the best You Tube music channel—bar none. Congratulations, Jim!

> Your name still is Jim, isn't it?

> Hey Steve, I got a story to tell you about Ray Charles that you just won't believe. 18 years ago I met Ray in a hospital. Let me start all over. I was in a car accident and was rushed to the hospital in Long Island. Well when I got there right next to me was the man himself, Ray Charles. He looked so dapper but was in bad shape. He was coming from a concert and his driver hit a tree and they rushed Ray to the hospital. The doctor told him that they were going to have to amputate his left leg that was terrible news, I wanted to cry. But then the doctor said "but you got the right one baby, uh huh. Enjoy Ray and America, The Beautiful!!

Other books written by author Jimmy Correa

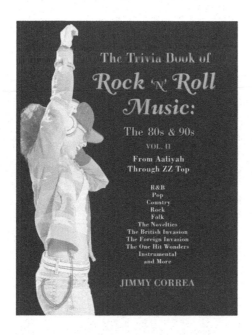

[Papcrback]
iUniverse

The Trivia Book of
Rock 'n' Roll Music:
VOL. I
The '50s, '60s, & '70s

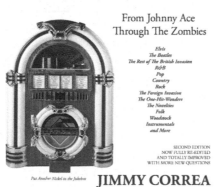

[Paperback]
iUniverse